O'CLOCK

Per a Joan Ramon,

Un primer vot
pels teus futurs cursos
de literatura catalana,
i una primera mostra
de sincera amistat.
Rep una forta abraçada de

Marta Camus

2 d'octubre 1986, Williamstown

Cover design by Bill Toth.
Book design by Iris Bass.
Author photograph by Ferran Sendra.

O'CLOCK

QUIM MONZÓ

Translated by
Mary Ann Newman

AVAILABLE
PRESS

BALLANTINE BOOKS • NEW YORK

My greatest appreciation to Ralph Tachuk for
his meticulous reading and warm support.

An Available Press Book

Translation copyright © 1986 by Mary Ann Newman

Library of Congress Catalog Card Number: 85-91528

ISBN 0-345-31668-1

Manufactured in the United States of America

First Edition: April 1986

CONTENTS

"I am proud to say that all my life I have been combating the ideas I am now defending."

"I am proud to respond that I find myself in exactly the opposite position."

Wolinski, in issue 436 of Charlie Hebdo.

Two Jews run into each other on a train in Galicia.

"Where are you going?" asks one.

"To Cracow," responds the other.

"You're a liar!" cries the first, enraged. "If you say you're on your way to Cracow it's because you want me to think you're on your way to Lemberg. But I know you're really on your way to Cracow. So, why did you lie to me?"

Quoted by Sigmund Freud in Jokes and Their Connection With the Unconscious.

COMPOSITION: What I Did on Sunday

SUNDAY WAS A VERY SUNNY DAY, AND I WENT OUT FOR A WALK with Mommy and Daddy. Mommy was wearing a beige dress, with an eggshell-colored cardigan, and Daddy an RAF-blue pullover and gray pants and a white shirt, open at the neck. I had on a turtleneck sweater, blue like Daddy's pullover, but lighter, and a brown jacket and brown pants, a little lighter than the jacket, and red sneakers. Mommy was wearing light-colored shoes and Daddy black ones. We walked around in the morning and went for breakfast at the Balmoral. We had hot chocolate with whipped cream and sweet rolls, and I ordered croissants. Then we looked at the flowers, and there were red and yellow and white and pink ones, and even blue ones, which Daddy said were dyed, and green plants and violets and big birds and little ones, and Daddy bought the paper at a newsstand. We also went window shopping, and Daddy told Mommy to hurry it up once when we spent a long time in front of a window with sweaters.

And then we sat on a green bench in a park, and there was an old woman with white hair and very red cheeks, like tomatoes, who was giving birdseed to the pigeons, and she reminded me of Grandma, and Daddy read the paper the whole time and I asked for the funnies and he gave me half the paper and told me not to mess it up.

On the way home Mommy told Daddy, 'cause he was reading the paper the whole time, that she was fed up, and she told him he was always reading it and that she was fed up, 'cause he read it at home, at breakfast, during lunch, in the street, walking, or in a cafeteria, or when we were out for a stroll. And Daddy didn't say a word and went on reading, and Mommy called him a name and then it seemed as if she was sorry, and she gave me a kiss and later, while Mommy was in the kitchen preparing lunch, Daddy told me not to pay any attention to her. We had rice with sauce, which I don't like, and meat with fried peppers. I really like the fried peppers, but not the meat, 'cause it's too rare, even though Mommy says it's better that way, but I don't like it. I like the meat they give us at school better, nice and dark. But at school I never like the first course, never. On the other hand, at home they give me wine with soda. And at school they don't. Later on in the afternoon my aunt and uncle came over with my cousin, and my aunt and uncle stayed in the living room with my parents, chatting and drinking coffee, and my cousin and I went to play in the yard. We played toy soldiers and catch and stickball. We played with the fire truck, and then we played war between the astronauts, and my cousin got all stupid 'cause he was losing, and the thing is my cousin really bothers me 'cause he doesn't know how to lose, so I had to give him a good smack, and he started crying real, real hard and Mommy came out and so did my aunt and my uncle, and Mommy said what happened, and before I could answer her my cousin said he hit me, and Mommy walloped me and I started crying too and we all went into the living room and Mommy took me by the hand and Daddy was reading the newspaper and smoking a cigar my uncle had brought him, and Mommy told him the kids are in the yard killing each other and here you sit back in your chair like a king. My aunt said it didn't matter,

but Mommy told her it was always like that, and that sometimes she just got fed up. Then my aunt and uncle left, and as
they were leaving my cousin stuck out his tongue at me, and I
stuck mine out at him, and Daddy turned on the television,
and there was a soccer game, and Mommy said to change the
channel, 'cause on the other station there was a movie, and
Daddy said no, 'cause he was watching the match, so no.

Then I went out to the yard, to see the doll I have buried
next to the tree, and I dug her up and I caressed her and I
scolded her because she hadn't washed her hands before lunch
and then I buried her again, and went out to the kitchen, and
Mommy was crying, and I told her not to cry. Then I went and
sat on the sofa next to Daddy and I watched the match for a
while, but soon I got bored and I looked at Daddy, and he didn't
look like he was watching the match either—like he was far
off somewhere or thinking real hard. Then the commercials came
on, which is what I like best, and then the second half, and I
went out to see Mommy, who was preparing supper, and then
we had supper and they showed cartoons and the news and an
old movie with an actress whose name I don't know who was
blond and very pretty and very busty. But then they made me
go to bed because it was late and I went upstairs and went to
bed and from the bed I could hear the movie and I heard how
my parents were fighting and arguing, but with the noise of the
television I couldn't exactly hear what they were saying. Then
they were shouting at the top of their lungs and I got out of bed
to get close to the door and hear what they were saying, but
since it was dark I couldn't see very well 'cause the only light
was from the moon coming in the window over the yard, and
since I couldn't see, I tripped and had to go back to bed, scared
that they might come and see what the noise had been, but
they didn't come. I could still hear them fighting. Now I could
hear it better because they had turned off the television, and
Daddy told Mommy not to bother him and called her names and
told her she had no purpose in life and Mommy called him
names back and told him to get out, and said a woman's name
and called her names, and then I heard something made of glass
break and then the cries were louder, and they were so loud I

couldn't understand them, and then I heard one loud scream, very loud, and then I didn't hear a thing. Then I heard another sound, soft, as if someone were dragging the ottoman around. I heard the door to the yard open and then I got out of bed again and heard noise outside and looked out the window and my feet were cold 'cause I wasn't wearing slippers. Outside it was dark and I couldn't see a thing and it sounded like Daddy was digging next to the tree and I was afraid he would find the doll and punish me so I got back into bed and covered myself all the way up, even my face, hidden beneath the sheets and everything dark and with my eyes shut tight. First I heard them stop digging and then footsteps going up the stairs and I pretended to be asleep, and I heard the door to my room open and I thought they must be looking at me, but I didn't see who it was because I was pretending to be asleep, so I couldn't see. Then they closed the door and I fell asleep and the next day, yesterday, Daddy told me Mommy had left home and then some men came and asked questions and I didn't know what to tell them and I cried the whole time and they took me to live with my aunt and uncle and my cousin always hits me, but that wasn't Sunday anymore.

THOMSON, BRAUN, CORBERÓ, PHILISHAVE . . .

To messrs. Justerini & Brooks, with gratitude

As soon as he closed the door, Pol felt relieved. It had been a more tiring trip than usual, everyone seemingly intent on inventing unnecessary obstacles. He hung up his raincoat (and the dust on the hanger reminded him that he had to clean the apartment), pushed the start button on the generator, opened the water valve, turned on a few lights around the house and checked out each of the rooms. He drew the curtains in the living room: In the midst of a ring of snowcapped mountains the village nestled deep in the valley like a crêche.

He found some cognac on a shelf. He took a swallow. He left the typewriter in its case and the briefcase with his papers and books on the table. The only thing he unpacked was a bag of shrimp, which he left on the marble countertop in the kitchen. He felt like the ass in the folktale: He was just as anxious to

start writing as he was to fix lunch. He went into the laundry
room to turn on the gas and heat. He tried to light the pilot
three times, but couldn't get the flame to catch. Just in case he
had forgotten, he read the instructions etched on the button: 1.
*Ouvrir le robinet d'arrêt gas situé au bas de l'appareil. 2. Pousser
ce bouton ā fond et tourner vers la droite. Allumer la veilleuse. Attendre
environ 15 secondes. Pousser de nouveau ā fond en tournant vers la
gauche puis relâcher.* The robinet d'arrêt gas was already open.
He pushed ce bouton ā fond once more and turned it to the
left. Slowly, he let it relâcher. The flame went out again.

He decided to give it a little rest. Out in the kitchen, he put a
few jars away and plugged in the refrigerator. He filled the ice
trays with water and put the shrimp on one of the shelves. He
picked up some empty bottles and left them in a straw basket.
Everything was covered with dust. In the living room, he took
the drop cloths off the couches, swept up and ran a dustcloth
over the furniture. In the bedroom, he got clean sheets out of
the closet, turned the mattress over and made the bed. He also
swept the study and dusted the books.

By midafternoon he realized that, in bustling about, he had
lost his appetite and forgotten to have lunch. He decided to fix
the jambalaya for dinner. All the cleaning had left him feeling
dirty; he needed a shower. Out in the laundry room, he tried
to light the heater again. He pressed the button in as far as it
would go, turned it to the right and released it, then he pushed it
again and turned it back to its original position. He let go very
gently; the flame disappeared. He tried four more times, with
the same luck. The heater was broken.

He had to take a cold shower (and felt like a fool, seeing nothing but snow out the window). He got dressed, picked up the
basketful of bottles, and went into town. He bought butter, milk,
ham, green peppers, tomatoes, onions, garlic, parsley, and bread.
He couldn't find Worcestershire sauce anywhere and it was clear
to him that he should have brought it from the city just as he
had done with the shrimp. He figured he could use soy sauce
(which the town supermarket had a good stock of) and vinegar as a substitute.

At the bar, he had a snack (less out of hunger than as a way

of asking the owner if he knew anyone who could fix his heater;
now he felt dirty inside, and he thought of ordering some mineral water). The owner did know someone who could, but who
happened to be away at the moment and wouldn't be back till
the following day. No need to worry, he would take care of
everything. It would be fixed the following morning, as soon as
the local mechanic arrived.

Back home, he put his purchases away. He took the typewriter out of its case and placed it in the middle of the table.
He put the stack of blank paper on the right; on the left, the
books he would need. Out the window (it was rapidly getting
dark) the snow was milky blue and the sky ashen. Since he'd
had a snack in the late afternoon he decided to start preparing
supper at nine. He had a couple of hours to write, so he got
started.

Sooner or later—and always half empty—page after page ended
up in the wastebasket. He pushed the machine away and lit a
cigarette. In town only a few lights were on: none of the stores;
only the lights from the bar, yellow, and the discotheque. He
felt a Siberian frost creeping up his spine. Without much hope,
he tried turning on the heater once again. He repeated each
step twenty times. Finally he slammed his fist into it. He remembered how when he was a kid his father had always gotten a Japanese transistor going (the first transistor he had ever
seen) by giving it a good punch. Perhaps the heater (though
not Japanese, nonetheless French) required similar treatment. He
punched the machine again, harder this time. The metal squeaked
and the machinery seemed to groan. Newly hopeful, he ran
through the procedure once again. But when the time came to
relâcher the bouton, the pilot light went out.

He slammed the machine once more, this time so hard that
the metal plate reading Chaffoteaux et Maury fell to the floor.
He had dented the side of it and the noise was getting progressively louder. Keeping his face as far back as he could, he repeated the whole operation in a state of mind that combined his
hope for a warm night with his fear of an explosion that might
take his head with it. This time when he let go of the button,
the pilot stayed lit, as if it were the simplest thing in the world.

He was annoyed, because he felt that all along he must have been
doing something wrong, if this time it had been so easy. He
took a look at the dented surface and picked up the metal plate.
He turned on all the radiators.

Feeling more relaxed, he turned on the television. Lines appeared. He tried moving the antenna. The lines turned into a
network of spots that jiggled constantly, like sleet. He remembered that the reception was very bad up there. He turned the
dial (wondering whether dial was the right word for the button
on the television set that serves the same purpose as the dial
on a radio). Finally, he felt that the picture was, if not good, at
least acceptable, given the conditions and the place. Then he
realized that they were broadcasting a soccer match, a spectacle
he found not only unappealing but deeply depressing. He pressed
the button for UHF. The screen was slashed by oblique lines.
He ran through the whole routine again, trying to adjust the
picture, but UHF was much more elusive than the other Spanish channel. A French voice came on suddenly, reminding him
that, up there, it would be easier to get French TV on VHF than
on UHF. He switched back. He ignored the Spanish broadcast
and tried to hunt down the froggy one, but it refused to appear.
Little by little, amidst a blizzard of fog, a girl's face emerged
(but faded away as soon as he moved the button even a smid-
gen). He searched for her stubbornly, but she never reap-
peared; now there was a fat emcee hugging a gangster type—who
must have been a singer—and presenting him with a horrible
little statuette. They were moving their lips, but the only thing
he could hear was fried noise. He moved the dial very slowly;
he picked up the sound, very faint. They were speaking Italian,
with neither subtitles nor translations. He was baffled. He tried
to tune in the picture, but when the picture cleared up the sound
disappeared, and when the sound cleared up then the picture
came down with the measles. Finally he found a middle ground
that satisfied him. The emcee signed off in Italian; the commercials were also in Italian. His last doubts were dispelled: He
was in the presence of Italian television. (Once he had managed to tune it in from the beach, during the summer on a very
clear day, but way up in the mountains in midwinter, with the

threat of a snowstorm hovering in the air . . .) He poured another cognac and felt quite pleased with himself. He drank it
down in two gulps. It was very cold. He feared the worst. He
got up in a flash and rushed over to the heater. The light
was on. He breathed a sigh of relief. He checked the rooms: The
radiators were cold.

As he walked by the television set, he saw Ornella Vanoni singing some Brazilian stuff. He got a move on. He looked at the
heater. He wondered if the water was too low. (Or too high?)
He opened the valve and the needle started to move slowly up-
ward: 1, 2 . . . Between the 4 and the 5 there was a red line that
seemed for all the world to want to indicate danger. The monster's bowels began to rumble. It seemed as though the heat should
start coming up any second. He increased the flow. The needle
hit the 3. He closed the valve. The needle continued to rise for a
few seconds. It stopped a bit above the 4. He made sure the
valve was shut tight. The needle wavered a hair's breadth away
from the red line. The monster's roar had gone up the scale to
a shrill whistle, then the gas caught and the flame spread across
the burner. The heater began to work.

He checked the radiators one by one. They were cold, but from
the symphony the pipes were producing it seemed clear that
the house would soon border on paradise. Meanwhile he headed
back to the television: Ornella Vanoni smiled and waved. The
fat emcee hugged her, handed her another statuette, and an-
nounced a brief pause, which Pol took advantage of to check
the radiators again. Of the six in the house, four were already
warming up. One of the two that weren't was in the foyer;
that one didn't matter. But the other was in the bedroom. He
looked to see if the knob was in the "on" position. It was. He
tried to unscrew the knob. He looked for a screwdriver, but the
one he found was too small. He gave the knob a sharp twist.
The screwdriver bent like a toy, but he had managed to strip
the threads and the knob was turning. When he took it off,
water streamed out as if shooting from a high pressure hose.

He was soaked from head to toe. The bed was soaked and the
floor was transformed into a pool in a matter of seconds. He was
hard put to replace the knob, but he finally did so, and in the

process splashed the walls that thus far had escaped being
drenched. He screwed it on and left it in place, dripping, with
the radiator off. He listlessly took off his wet clothes and changed
into his pajamas. He mopped the floor, then stripped the bed
and stretched the blankets and sheets out all over the house.
He considered his options: He could shut the water off and fix
the radiator (but it had been so hard to get the heater going
that he didn't want to run the risk of its putting another one
over on him). He decided to write the radiator off. He would
wait for the whiz kid the owner of the bar had promised him
for the following day. In the meantime, he would sleep in the
bed—with extra blankets—or in the living room in the sleeping
bag. He took another look at the heater. It was in perfect working order.

On the television, a black trio was singing. He looked out the
window. The bar was now closed and except for the discotheque the whole town was dark. He thought of getting up and
going to bed. He had had a pretty harrowing day. If he went
to bed early, he'd be able to work steadily the next day. He was
sorry, though, about losing the Italian station (perhaps irre-
trievably) and having to postpone the jambalaya. Undecided, he
curled up on the sofa. Within fifteen minutes, he was sound
asleep and dreaming of feasts with laden tables in the sun-
drenched gardens of New Orleans (on the street, trams were
rattling along on tracks sketched through the grass and the trees).
When the time came to be served, the chefs were shouting in-
dignantly and he, having just arrived, felt guilty about being late
and ran off under ironwork balconies, not knowing where the
sauce was hidden. The chefs laughed in silence ...

He was awakened by the absence of noise. The television screen
was blank, and he turned it off. He was as hungry as he was
tired. In the kitchen, he heard a faint dripping that wasn't coming from any faucet. It was the refrigerator, which had broken
down. The scant amount of ice that had formed in the short time
it had been on was slowly melting. He unplugged it. With what
seemed to him to be a titanic effort, he turned it around. He
couldn't make heads or tails of the hieroglyphic wiring. He
pushed the refrigerator back in place and plugged it in again.

Not even the light bulb went on. Before leaving the kitchen he went out to the laundry room and looked at the heater again: The flame was right in place.

He got a sleeping bag out of the closet. He slid in and lay on the parquet right next to the radiator. He tossed and turned, unable to find a good position. He wondered whether it wouldn't have been better to turn the mattress over and sleep on it. Maybe it wasn't so wet as he had first thought. But he didn't have the strength to get up.

Forty-five minutes later, he admitted that he couldn't sleep. Out in the kitchen, he fixed himself a few slices of bread with oil and sugar. He ate them. He sat down at the typewriter and began to write. He wrote half a page and ripped it out of the machine. He crumpled it up into a ball and threw it into the wastebasket. In the kitchen, he sliced some bread and pro-sciutto and ate it. He took *Candide ou l'optimisme* out of his bag. He read it, sitting on a chair in the kitchen.

The lights took exactly thirteen minutes to go out. By candle-light, he checked the fuses. They seemed fine. He looked out the window. The fact that there wasn't a single light out there didn't prove a thing; it was logical at four-thirty in the morning. He lighted more candles and went on reading.

When he woke up it was daylight. He had fallen asleep at the table and was frozen. He yawned and his bones felt ready to shatter into icicles. He felt the radiators; they were all cold. He ran to the heater; the flame was in place, but the thermostat read zero. He turned the water up—3, 4, 4½ . . . He left the red line behind. The excess water began flowing from a tube jutting out from the building. The heater groaned, the light seemed about to catch on the burner, but in the end it went out.

He thought of making some coffee. When he found the cof-fee mill full of whole beans, he remembered that it had been broken since his last visit. He found a pot and poured milk into it. Then he had a better idea: He left the pot of milk on the marble counter and looked for a pot and a pan. He turned on the stove (at least the stove was working). He cleaned and boiled the shrimp. Then he put a pan on the fire and added butter.

The prosciutto followed in large cubes, along with finely chopped green pepper. He stirred this for a few minutes and, without stopping, added a little flour. A minute later, he added the shrimp, water, quartered tomatoes, minced onion, garlic, and parsley. When it started to boil he added rice, salt, thyme, red pepper, soy sauce, and vinegar. He covered it and turned down the flame. For half an hour he kept watch as it simmered.

There was a knock at the door: The guy at the bar had sent a mere child to fix the heater. Pol showed him not only the heater, but the whole gamut of gadgets that needed fixing, and the radiators: one by one. He took too long to explain. He realized this when he poured out the jambalaya. It had stuck to the bottom of the pan and the only thing he could salvage was a colorless paste, which bore scant likeness to a gastronomic treat.

He picked up the pot of milk and put it on the stove. The boy called him over to explain how easy it was not to break the radiator if, from the very start, you twisted the knob in the right direction. He got back to the kitchen too late: the milk had boiled over and flooded all four burners. Phlegmatically he guzzled his milk straight from the bottle. He stuck two slices of bread in the toaster. They came out charcoal gray.

He hid in the bathroom. He vowed firmly not to come out until all the machines within the radius of a kilometer were repaired. He pulled the chain and it broke in three places. He looked at himself in the mirror and saw a spirit in flight with five o'clock shadow. On the verge of making the worst mistake of his life, he looked at the electric shaver in his hand. He panicked and threw it into the bidet: He had seen its fangs.

Outside, the boy was waiting. Together they ascertained that the heater, the radiators, the coffee grinder, the refrigerator, and the toaster were in perfect working order. Just in case, they had a look at the shaver. There was nothing wrong with it. They replaced the broken chain with a piece of string until he could buy another. Pol paid the boy and off he went.

After shaving, he sat down at the Olivetti. Smoke was streaming out of his ears: He had been frenzied all the way up with the desire to get there and start writing. Having placed too much confidence in a too-weak memory, he hadn't made note of any of the thousands of ideas that had flooded his brain. Unfortunately, he hadn't been able to call up a single image since he had reached the house. He was blank and didn't know what to say. All the radiators were now going at full tilt, and the house was filling with an overwhelming heat. He lit a cigarette. He started typing. He knew almost immediately what he should write about: Precisely the chain of wretched circumstance that had plagued him for the last twenty hours. The lines flowed right along: *It had been a more tiring trip than usual, everyone seemingly intent on inventing unnecessary obstacles. . . .* Then he stopped: The sun was aflame outside. He was sweating. He took off his sweater and went out to the laundry room to turn off the heater. He didn't feel the slightest fear that this gesture might be irreversible. Back at the table, he reread what he had written: *He tried once more to light the heater. He pressed the button as far as it would go, turned it to the right and released it. . . .* Now he knew that the more lines he wrote, the more relaxed he would feel. He had to get it all down: From the time he left the city till the arrival of the mere child; even longer, till this very moment in which, restored to normalcy, he sat at the typewriter untying the knot. Only then, emptied of all his grief, would he begin to write what he had really come up there to hide out and write, and all the ideas that had bombarded him during the trip would appear in perfect order: effortlessly he would fill the sheets of paper in the pile to his right with thick stripes; and when they were all full, he would go down to the village and buy a bottle of Alella wine to accompany the unsurpassable jambalaya that he would prepare soon thereafter. . . . But suddenly a key from the Olivetti sprang into the air in an acrobatic leap. Within seconds, the typewriter was totally dismantled; hopelessly reduced to a heap of bolts, bars, and springs.

APPLE PEACH

I CAN'T EVEN RECOUNT THE PLOT OF THE FILM. I ONLY REMEMber (very vaguely) that it was full of cheap stunts and cardboard chases. Every so often the leading lady would fall down with a plateful of spaghetti or an equivocal situation would catch the male lead in his underwear. The audience laughed, not because the picture was funny, but because it was so stupid as to be grotesque. In the back rows, they began to kid around and started a running commentary that had it all over the on-screen dialogue.

I first saw her when I took a look at the people around me: a dark profile eating peanuts, throwing the shells on the floor. She coughed once, looked over her shoulder once (but not at me, or at anyone in particular) and yawned, like everyone else, when she left.

By midafternoon, I was sick of wandering through bookstores. I had tried, to no avail, to lift a book (when I fail in these undertakings I am progressively consumed by depression, beset by thoughts of suicide). On the verge of pocketing a trigonometry text (the only thing within reach in the only secluded corner of the bookstore), I saw her again. Now she had on yellow glasses and her glance of approval made me wonder whether she recognized me from earlier that day or just sympathized with my kleptomaniacal sufferings. For a second, I thought it was a look of accusation.

Needless to say, when I saw her again (that same night, two tables down in an exotic restaurant, dressed in black and caressing the hand of an overly cold and distant man), it was already absurdly obvious to me that not only would I run into her again the following day (at the theater), but for the entire coming week we would be bumping into each other on the street, in bars, and in movie houses. She would, of course, affect amnesia, bent on acting out a series of diverse roles. Finally (at a cocktail party at the opening of an utterly insignificant sculpture exhibit), a mutual friend introduced us. She denied ever having seen me before, which (although at first I attributed it to a stubborn effort to belittle me) was quite disconcerting in the end, in light of her inviting attitude. We had dinner and—so as not to turn this into a pornographic tale—I need only say that, when I awakened, she was gone. Just a note: "I'll be calling you. Hugs and kisses."

She didn't call that morning. That same afternoon (while I looked at chocolates in a shop window), she passed by without seeing me, a real beauty in black shorts. "You mean to say you don't recognize me?" I protested, pinching her behind. In her amazement, she left the mark of four of her five fingers painted across my cheek. She called me a shameless and insolent bum, an opinion in obvious contradiction to her claim of never having seen me in her life. Finding myself the object of insults and potshots from everyone in sight (all of whom rapidly took her side), I managed to make my way into a side street where (even more disconcertingly) I saw her again, this time in an outrageous blouse and very tight skirt. She asked, with a smile, if I was going her way and when I asked where that might be (a perfectly idiotic question warranted only by my bewilderment

at her inexplicable change in dress), she said, somewhat ironi-
cally, to pick cherries, if I was interested. By that point, the
only thing I was interested in was losing her, it didn't matter
how, and I managed to do so by running toward the boule-
vard. But things had become all too clear: She was there, too,
dressed in blue and sitting on a bench, which was no mean feat
since, at that precise moment, a few yards farther on, she was
also buying an ice cream, in white jeans.

By nightfall, she was everywhere: Either all the women were
wearing her face or her face was reproduced on all their faces,
under a moon which, like everything else around me, ran on in
infinite Xerox copies until the sky seemed to resemble an IBM
card. By then it didn't take a lot of intelligence to predict my
own future, to guess the next step in that cosmic conspiracy.
When I stopped to look at a circus poster, the other man looking at it turned to me at the same time I turned to him and
for a moment I didn't know which side of the mirror I was on.
Another me outside of me was observing me with surprise, not
quite understanding why I was taking the knife out of my pocket,
still doubtful as to whether, on sinking it into his chest (his
chest and all the other chests which, like his, were mine without
being mine), I wasn't actually driving it into my own.

THE SALMON LADY

THE FIRST THING I FELL IN LOVE WITH WAS THE WAY SHE crossed her legs. Very gently, as if she were afraid of breaking them, as if they were made of ice. She raised one and slipped it over the other, both legs pressed together from knee to ankle. That was my *madeleine*. Suddenly my head was full of a skein of images of aunts and cousins, and sepia photographs of a 1920s' grandmother wearing a round hat and a short skirt, her legs pressed together in just the same way as my traveling companion's in that compartment. Then, after a while, she uncrossed them by extending one of them forward in such a way that for a second the entire leg (from pubis to foot) was perfectly straight. Once they were parallel, she shifted both perfect and splendid salmon-toned specimens to one side. A pair of legs like that could make for the total happiness of whomsoever might share in them (and to share them would be to observe them endlessly, caress them day and night, bare under the silk of her stockings).

Those legs could bring disgrace and suicide upon the man who lost them ... could unleash infinite wars—a new Helen of Troy with the legs of Marlene Dietrich, staring out the window at the interminable stretch of green fields and scattered houses backed by a drapery of trees, half ochre and half white.

In Hønefoss the train stopped for a long time. They made us get off. I couldn't understand why we had to change cars, but since no one complained I saw no reason to doubt the company's good intentions. The cars we had been traveling in quickly disappeared into the distance and five minutes later their replacements appeared.

The passengers all hurried aboard and sat wherever they could. As I had lost all hope of continuing to contemplate the lady's legwork, I set out toward one of the last cars. I found an empty compartment and settled in. I took the blue guide out of my bag and became absorbed in the perusal of altitudes, villages, and restaurant possibilities. My peace soon came to an end: Someone opened the door of the compartment and from that moment on I was surrounded by a muffled but continuous racket of packages and kids. Nose buried in the book, I tried to lose myself in details of the quality of the salmon on the islands off the coast. The feeling that I was being watched distracted me, and I raised my head. Across from me, a child was demanding to be read a comic book by a woman who seemed to be his mother and really not up to the task. I ran my gaze vaguely about the compartment: Right next to me sat that splendid woman, the one with the fancy legs.

I was shocked. (While there were still other seats in the compartment, she had chosen precisely the seat next to mine!) I looked at her out of the corner of my eye. She stared straight ahead, apparently at the child who was insisting that his mother read him the story. I opened the guide. Herring ...

In Sokna, mother and child got off and an old man got on. No sooner had the train left the station than I felt a pressure on my leg. She (the lady with the salmon-colored legs) was rubbing one of hers against one of mine! It didn't take me long to react. Not only did I accede to her caress, I returned it. Out of the corner of my eye I thought I saw her smile. Now what should I do? I entertained the hope that the old man might get off at the next stop, leaving us to ourselves. But a whole slew of stations went by and the old man didn't move. His eyes were closed and his head was propped up against one of the headrests. He slept so soundly, in such blank silence, that I wondered if he hadn't died. What if he had missed his stop? Perhaps it would be an act of kindness to awaken him. Cautious foreigner that I was, I preferred to keep my peace; all the more so since the population of our compartment had now increased by one: a girl some twenty years of age with an oversized bag and huge transparent eyes.

The woman's leg and mine went on in Siamese splendor, but apparently neither of us was clever enough to figure out an outlet for our desires. When the train had been well under way for some time, I gathered up the courage to ask her if she was going far. At first she didn't even look at me. When I repeated the question, she turned (at which point, from so close up, I was able to perceive that she was a mature beauty), smiled with bloodtinged lips, and responded in Norwegian. (My hope that she might belong to that considerable portion of the population that has English as its second tongue were dashed at one blow.) I was brought up short. She tacked on another phrase and was perhaps awaiting a response that I couldn't offer. The younger woman was reading a fashion magazine and seemed totally detached from the world around her. But the old man who had appeared almost dead in his sleep opened his eyes and translated for me: The lady expressed her regrets at not speaking my language. I thought of telling her that it was not my language, but merely one that I had borrowed. The old man offered to continue his services as translator. I became flustered (imagining myself down on one knee, declaring my love through an interpreter). I didn't know how to go on, so I politely said no thank you to the old man. A slightly touchy silence ensued. (Our legs, however, were still fused.) The old man closed his eyes again, but not for long: When we pulled into Torpo, he said good-bye and got off.

Between Torpo and Ål, I slowly let my hand slip over hers, stroking the back of it with my fingertips. I thought I saw her eyelids flutter. She shifted her arm in such a way that, interlaced, our hands were closed tight as a nutshell. The girl across from us was noisily flipping pages and looking out the window every so often. She abruptly closed the magazine and dropped it on the seat next to her. Her glance fell upon our two hands for a second and, suddenly discreet, she examined her bag, tightened one of its straps, became absorbed once again in the passing scenery, and yawned.

It seemed as if night would never fall. A middle-aged man in a green uniform who looked like a forest ranger boarded at Geilo. All opportunities were now set to flight. I made a decision: I would get up with the woman's hand tightly grasped in mine and go out into the passageway where at least we would be able to communicate a little better, if not quite carry on a conversation. The risk, though, was in the possibility of her not going along with the game and saying something that I wouldn't be able to understand (but that the other occupants of the compartment would). In my favor was the fact that, in truth, she had been the one to take the initiative and that my advance (taking her hand) had certainly not been rejected. It perturbed me, though, that she might not be aware of my unfortunate situation, a stranger in a cold land. As she was the one playing on home ground, it was up to her to decide what came next. Or was she content just to hold hands and rub her leg against mine?

I stood up with her hand firmly clutched in mine. For a second I thought she wasn't going to follow suit. She looked at me in surprise. Then she smiled and led the way out the door. We walked down the passageway to the end of the car. On the platform, she started to utter very slow words which certainly must have seemed basic enough to her but were all Norwegian to me. (I realize that's not a very clever joke.) It was obvious that we must soon hit upon a tongue (and here I shall resist the facile pun) satisfactory to both of us. Slowly syllabifying, I laid my four language possibilities before her. She understood, because she then named three, which I also understood, much to my dismay (and hers, I imagine), as none of her three matched any of my four. How, then, was I to tell her I was mad about her legs; that I wanted to embrace her and caress her before

the time came for her to flee at some unforeseeable station; that
her decision to rub up against my leg was the most delightful
gesture anyone had made toward me in at least a week? We kissed
blindly (our first kiss; the overture to the symphony), in an embrace as long as the bridge we were crossing. This was brought
to an end by the opening of the door leading to the corridor:
The girl from our compartment was on her way to the bathroom which, I then realized, was right there on the platform
where we were wasting our time necking like schoolchildren without going on to more substantial acts. And as the girl closed the
bathroom door I remember thinking we needed only to wait for
her to come out to begin enjoying the fruits of that amorous
hideout being offered to us on a silver platter.

Ten minutes later, the girl had still not emerged. It aroused
me to wonder what delicious acts *she* might be engaged in. I
would have liked to insinuate as much to my unknown friend
who was by now bent on repeating words (perhaps of love, of
sexual frenzy?) in each of the languages she spoke, in the hope
that I would understand; it was no use. It was all glacial gargling
to me, echoes sounding in a fjord. And, out the window, snowcapped
plains.

Many minutes later, the conductor came by and asked for our
tickets. In our haste, we had left our bags in the compartment
and had to go back and get them. The forest ranger was no longer
there. The conductor did his job and left. We were alone again.
I had just begun to caress one of her knees when the girl came
in. So I imagined the bathroom must now be empty again. I
started to get up, but the woman said something and remained
seated. I must have looked perplexed, for the girl seemed to feel
obliged to translate for me: "She says she's getting off at the next
stop."

I got her suitcase down. The train came to a much noisier halt
than it had anywhere before. She gave me a good-bye kiss on
the cheek and added a few words. "She says," the girl translated, "that she's very sorry not to have met you in other, more
auspicious, circumstances." "Tell her I feel the same way," I said.
She translated. The woman of my dreams smiled and disappeared down the passageway.

I sat down for a mere two seconds, as I quickly said to myself that the world was not made for cowards. I picked up my bag and satchel and headed for the door. The girl, who seemed not to understand my purpose, stared at me, openmouthed. Down on the station platform, I felt lost. The woman was gone, there was no one there. I dashed into the station: empty. I went out front: there was a square with neon signs, but no people. Ten yards away from the door to the station my ex-seatmate, the lady of the salmon-colored skin, was hugging a man, kissing a child, and getting into a Volkswagen. I turned back at top speed. All I needed now was to miss the train! It was already moving out when I jumped on. I went back to my compartment. The girl was surprised. I put my satchel up on the shelf and took the blue guide out of my bag. The girl pulled her feet up on the seat, hugged her legs to her body and, looking straight at me, laughed with a laugh I took to mean something that later turned out to be wrong. She said: "I'm sorry to have broken up your little affair, but I had to hide out in the bathroom because I haven't got a ticket." Now she was sitting with her legs perfectly crossed; perfect, parallel, splendid legs . . .

Early that morning, she accidentally gave herself away: When she went to get her cigarettes out of the bag, her ticket fell to the floor. I pretended to be looking out the window.

CACOPHONY

A HAD ALWAYS HAD THE INSANE DESIRE TO DRIVE THE WRONG way up Balmes—either mistakenly (during a night on the town, when all the thrill spots were already shut down) or willfully (to shatter the opaque mirror of routine). He imagined growing waves of automobiles, colors at boiling point in irate mouths; frantic lights veering right and left to avoid him and (in consequence) crashing into one another; the greatest catastrophe in history; a concentric chaos spreading from street to street, from neighborhood to neighborhood, from city to city, opening its way from one continent to the next, to the sea . . .

He was feeling it now, this desire. Quite contrarily, however (and he clucked his tongue against his palate to cloak a green taste of bile), he started down Balmes according to the dictates of strictest orthodoxy: down toward the sea; he had just left La Rotonda behind. He had drunk gimlets on the skirt of the mountain amid palm trees, sitting in an unbleached canvas lounge chair in the exact spot where the last tram on the planet came full circle and an absent pianist, on the verge of expiring, picked out "Three Little Words" over and over again on a shiny black piano.

Down by Putget station, he had to slam on the brakes: a bum light. He turned on the radio. He twisted the dial. He chanced upon Benny Goodman, which lifted him into an optimism he considered excessive. He turned up the volume. The light turned green and reminded him of aniline dyes. He changed lanes on crossing Mitre. As if treading on dry leaves, he accelerated. Right across from the Crystal City bar/bookstore, he parked up on the sidewalk. He went in. There was a girl reading magazines at the bar. Only one table in the place was taken. He had a coffee, browsed through the bookshelves: from Euskera geographical treatises to enigmas of dust-blown Egypt. He leafed through *The Last Tycoon*. He took small sips. He paid for the book and the coffee. He went outside. He ran a red light on Via Augusta.

He felt very much alone, and thought of having a midnight snack. He looked at his watch. He wasn't supposed to meet up with B for another half hour. He lit a cigarette; he imagined himself smoking three. He lit up two more and smoked all three at once. He smiled to think how he must look from another car. He was pleased at the effect. He thought to himself that in this world no one thing was better than any other thing; he thought of streetlights falling to the ground, of streetlights sinking into the earth. He felt cold.

Before reaching Travessera he wondered whether to turn left and lose himself in Gràcia. He didn't come to a decision until La Granada and by then it was too late and his head was lost in new choices: Whether to park by Tuset and remember old times or eat an omelette ensconced in ugly white vinyl. At the light on the Diagonal he had the feeling he would be driving down that street forever.

He pulled out as soon as the pedestrians' green began to flicker. A car slowly making its way toward Macià swerved to avoid him, honked, cursed at him, and crashed into a garbage can. A accelerated, left streets and colorless streetlights behind (suddenly worried to think that perhaps the stoplights were in fact blind). He crossed Gran Via on red, brazenly (and caused two

collisions and injuries; the howling of an ambulance and a shooting star; but that was some minutes later). He saw the Forn
del Cigne locked tight. He wondered whether they were inside
preparing pastries at that hour. He thought of crashing in, breaking down the door, driving toward the back room, greeting the
bakers and leaving the place through the emergency exit, dust-
ing the flour off his sleeves. It wasn't true that he was going to
be driving down that street forever. He jumped the amber light
and continued down the Rambla. He parked at the door of the
Baviera. He sat down at a dirty, cold table on the sidewalk.
Not many passersby. He yawned.

B arrived late, in a white sweater and light blue pants. A vi-
sualized her ass, her underpants. He looked at his watch.

"Not very punctual."

"You just don't know how bad the traffic is. I came by cab
and we had to detour down to the Paral·lel, and crowds of
people were coming out of the theaters and the police were
rounding people up on Nou Street. They're nuts. They've closed
down the Marsella and the London. They didn't let us come down
the Rambla. I had to walk over from the cathedral . . .

A thought it must have been at least ten years since he had
last set foot in the London. He remembered a friend, a night
at the Enfants Terribles, the police station, the sweet-roll bakery
that opens in the wee hours. He was surprised at the passing
of time. B was still talking:

". . . as if they thought they could keep us in line. Just think—at
our age, now that each of us has a corner on his own small
parcel of truth. Don't pull that stupid face on me. Don't you realize everyone considers himself the navel of the earth? The
day before yesterday, Tèbia was telling me . . ."

A was thirsty. He signaled to a waiter who didn't so much as
glance at him. B's chattering was seamless:

". . . and Riba has money (and having money is the most important thing in the world to him, the only important thing),
and Joan fucks a different girl every night (because seducing a
different girl every night is the most important thing for him,
and he thinks that anyone who wastes his time in other endeav-
ors is short on brains), and Marcel eats a lot (and can't under-

stand how anyone can spend much time very far from a well-stocked
table), and . . ."

A decided to speed down the Rambla and drive into the water. The waiter was attending another party, three tables down.

". . . reads for days, and Manel is the *most* into amphetamines
of the whole group (the *most*, eh? Mr. Number One), and Marta
is an idiot (nothing less than the *biggest* idiot in the building:
Ms. Number One), and Pere and Núria are utterly in love (because they've seen a lot of Doris Day movies and they hold the
record as the most stable couple in the neighborhood), and Xa-
vier is very introverted (maybe the *biggest* loner of all the intro-
verts in the country) and Maria is the *most* extroverted . . ."

A lowered his head. He imagined his car skirting the sidewalk of the monument to Columbus, speeding toward the stairs
down to the port, B screaming, the car spinning uncontrollably,
flipping onto its side, falling gently into the oily water, opaque
with petroleum.

". . . Eugeni watches more TV than *anyone* in town (he holds
the *record*) and old Pere works the hardest (harder than anyone *else* at the shop), and Octavi drinks beyond all moderation
(and he's proud as punch to be the worst alcoholic in his house),
and Tomàs is a movie freak, and Manolo's in the vanguard of
the working class, and Ignàsia wants to change the system from
within, and Eulàlia's radical, and Artur's gay, and Mr. Jaume's
happy and heterosexual, and Andreu's a poet and Fina's always cold. Everything works out because everyone has a niche.
There's a behavior pattern for every last one of us; a hat for
every head, a navel . . ."

A seized his chance when B interrupted her lecture to take a
breath:

"We could go for a drink someplace else where they might
wait on us."

They got up as the waiter was coming toward them. He shot
them a look out of the corner of his eye and grumbled. They
got into the car. They drove around the plaza and went down
the Ronda de la Universitat. At Balmes, A braked. Now build-
ings as well as streetlights were sinking into the ground.

He turned right. So here he was, going up Balmes, and the

cries, laughter, and feeble objections of B blended with the razz-
ing of the people on the street, few and far between and looking
for a good show. When you go the wrong way on a one-way
street, thought A, there are no stoplights. He met his first car on
the other side of the Gran Via; the driver looked at them
in surprise. From there to the Diagonal, they came across seven
more (none of which had any difficulty in changing lanes). When
they reached Via Augusta they once again had the right-of-way,
finding themselves face-to-face with the stoplights again. They
went up Tibidabo Avenue and, on reaching the point where the
tram comes to rest, they found the bars closed. A thought it
was like cheating to have gone up Balmes so late at night, with
so few cars out. They parked and, leaning on a railing that faced
the void, watched the city that spilled over into (at the same time
that it was bound by) the sea, which knows no boundaries. Three
hours later, the sun began to come up little by little.

TWINS

HOW ABOUT A CUP OF TEA? LOOK, TANO, I'M GLAD YOU CAME over. I've been swamped these past few days, what with the whole to-do about my old maiden aunts and all. No one knows which end is up. And I'm still not completely out of the woods with Coia. I don't know ... we should have talked it over, you and I. Toward the end, before she ran off with you, that month between the time she met you and the time she left, our life was like an insane asylum—shouting, arguments ... you can't imagine what it was like, the constant tension. It was as if the world had been covered over with needles and everything was tottering—as if I were balanced on the edge of an abyss. One day, at the dinner table, she made a gesture that reminded me of one of yours, when we were kids at home: She picked up the bread knife and stared at me with such a serene hatred that I don't know what scared me more, her expression or the weapon she was brandishing. Or maybe it was finally realizing exactly how much in love with you she was, so much so that she had picked up your gestures, and had started talking like you. It was very clear to me that it was all over. That's the way it always goes; it's the little things that give you away. Or maybe more than just the little things—I mean the little things are just the tip of the iceberg. What you can't see is the larger picture. Another time, for example, I was in the bathtub, nice and relaxed, and she burst in, giving me hell (I can't recall what for) and carrying the electric heater in her hands. Before I had time to realize that, in point of fact, the wire was too short to reach all that way and still be plugged in, I had already leaped out of the tub and was crouched between the bathrobes, terrified. Just picture it—grotesque! So, she threw the heater into the tub, which made lots of smoke and fumes, and my would-be assassin turned on her heel and left. That's how things were going, you see. Every other day or so a similar scene would take place. I also did my share. By no means do I deny the streak of madness that runs through me. But as you well know, it's easier to talk about the foibles of others than about one's own. Those were very tense days—until she moved out. Later on, after some time had elapsed, we were able to talk calmly and we more or less cleared things up. But, I'm not sure you know about this next part: Two or three weeks later, when I was feeling most bitter about my loss, she phoned me. I, who had been struggling like a fool to rid myself of her memory, once again had her on my mind day and night. She suggested that we get together, one day when you weren't around—off on a trip somewhere. (You're no slouch, by the way, with these trips you dream up for yourself.) We went out for dinner. Me, I was out of control, chafing at the bit, my heart going a mile a minute, and the first thing she tells me is that the reason she called me was to start making arrangements for getting her things out of the house. She said it as a way of creating a distance, right from the start. You can just picture it (you know how I am); something cracked inside me. When they brought the sautéed veal, she said I seemed cold and distant. What did she expect, after treating me so coldly herself? Honestly, this game of now-you-have-me-now-you-don't—so typical of Coia—I'll just never understand it. And now you'll see what I mean: When the ice cream sundaes came she asked me if I wanted to sleep with her that night. Of course I did! I mean, I wanted not to want to, but I was delirious to be with her again, even if it was only for one night. Look, that's just the way things are. We came back here. When we got here, she put the Beatles on the record player and picked out a couple of LP's, which she decided I was going to lend her. "I'll return them to you in a couple of days," she said. In bed, after a little kissing and fondling, she told me in no uncertain terms that she didn't feel like fucking. When she saw that I was up like the Tower of Pisa, she felt guilty. "You see? I shouldn't have asked if you wanted to sleep with me." She decided she would masturbate me. But her hand got tired in no time and she let the whole thing slide. I went out to the kitchen to grab a whiskey, and when I got back to bed, she was sound asleep. The next morning, I got up early and left without waking her. When I got home that evening I found a note in which she proposed that we get together another day and thanked me for lending her the records. Ten days later she called. You were who-knows-where again. We went out for dinner and this time we went dancing afterward, and we were clinging to each other the whole time with an intensity ... I'll spare you the details; you know well enough how Coia is. Well, when we stopped dancing, she goes and tells me that she has to get up early the next day and that she'll call me again the next time she has nothing to do. Taken by surprise, I barely had time to remind her that she had a few records to return. She didn't telephone me for two more weeks. One evening I was in bed with Tèbia, with whom I was trying to fall in love again. (She had been my fiancée before I met Coia. You met her once—when we were on our way out of a movie theater one New Year's Eve.) So Coia says to me, "Have you forgotten that tomorrow is your birthday?" Of course, I remembered—with some sadness, however, since my birthday is also yours, wretched fate, whereby on the same day that I, the previous two years, had blown out the candles by her side, this year you were to be blowing them out by her side. Coia was insistent. It appeared that you would both be truly pleased if we all spent our joint birthday together. I wasn't clever

enough to pick up on the depravity of it all, but I'm just that
kind of fool: I thought you were doing it so I wouldn't feel so
lonely. You know how it is; I always trip over the same old stone.
I don't know how to see people's fangs. She offered to drive
by and pick me up and then take me home after dinner. There
was no saying no. The following day she came to pick me up.
In the car, she was all kisses, hugs, caresses that left me ... Once
home—I mean your home—you know very well what hap-
pened. We had a few martinis, you two started right up, and by
dessert time you were rolling around on the carpet. I felt you
had invited me to play the role of the reluctant voyeur. I didn't
like the situation and I left. The following day, Coia called me:
"Are you angry?" I told her I wasn't—which, by the way, was
true. I hadn't gotten angry, I had left. I had had two choices:
getting angry or leaving. I had chosen the second. Fair enough?
Coia persisted: "But you're hurt, aren't you?" She went on and
on. I suppose she expected me to say yes by wearing me down.
To cut her off, I told her we'd have to start thinking about
the details of our separation. She remembered that she owed me
some records, which she promised to return shortly. I rarely
left the house those days. I was trying to forget Coia and fall in
love with Tèbia again, as I've already told you. But I don't know
... with all the anxiety about not living with her, yet seeing her
from time to time, and talking with her on the phone, I still
haven't been able to forget her. And all this despite the fact that
since she's been with you she's changed a lot, and that ought
to bother me. In fact, it bothers me a great deal, as is only natural. Do you remember the time when we were little that I took
the cardboard horse the little girl who lived next door (what was
her name?) had given you? I've thought a lot about that lately.
You said you'd get back at me, and I was really scared of the
way you said it, because you said it very seriously. Of course,
kids rarely say anything totally seriously. But you were never much
of a kid. Before you were a foot tall you were acting like an
adult. What I don't remember is how I got that horse, or even
whether I grabbed it for just a moment or took it off somewhere with me. If I only snitched it from you for a moment,
then you really overreacted. You've always been very impul-

sive. In time, you learned to feign goodness and play dirty tricks on me behind my back. You cooked up the most elaborate schemes and arranged it so that I would suffer the consequences. You learned to put up a good front. How old were we when you forged the papers and sold Dad's car? Nineteen? And you arranged it so that I would look like the guilty one. It's a good thing that a month before Dad died he realized that you'd been putting one over on him all his life. He saw that I was the good kid and you the bad, in a manner of speaking. He left you without a dime. I think it must be the biggest comeuppance you've ever had. I only wish Coia would catch on to you, too. Fat chance! Do you know that the last time I saw her— some fifteen days ago—she was carrying an anthology of Russian liter- ature under her arm? You're eating away at her personality. And now, with all this to-do about the death of our maiden aunts, she hasn't even called me. And here you show up. You always appear when you're least expected. You know how I loved old Auntie Helena and Auntie Elisabet. Who's gone to visit them all these years? Not you. Surely you haven't come here with re- criminations. To a certain extent, it's logical that Auntie He- lena would remember me more than you. But talking about all this stirs up so many things in me. They died such a grue- some death—hatchet blows to the skull! Does it upset you to hear about it? No, of course not. I don't know why I should even think to ask you such a thing. Did you know that Auntie He- lena was just a couple of months away from retirement? It was a real shock to the people at the bank. They were very fond of her. It's not often that people are fond of their managers, right? But they were of her, that's a fact. They arrested two guys, but they've been released for lack of proof. They said they were going over to discuss a loan—to her home. Do you believe it? It's very strange. But the police say it wasn't them ... it looks as if they let them go because they've caught the real murderers. The papers haven't reported this yet, but it's two painters who were working on the second floor of her building. (Why are you laughing? You think that's funny? You have no heart.) They're still missing a few links, but now they're certain they've got them. And what about you? Tell me about yourself. I haven't let you open your mouth since you arrived. You hurt me very badly, going off with Coia. Do you love her? Sometimes I think you're not capable of loving anyone. Lately, things are going better and better with Tèbia. I don't think I would give her up for Coia anymore. Imagine us reaching the point of a falling-out over the same woman. Sometimes I think we're so alike physically that inevitably one has to irk the other. It's as if down there just one child should be born and no more. But since, unexpectedly, there were two of us—and the second could just as easily be one as the other, no one was keeping track—things won't be back to normal until one makes the other disappear. Finally there will be just one; one will have consumed the other. Our characters, on the other hand, couldn't be more different. Don't laugh. You've always been taciturn, and impulsive, and a reader. How's your honors thesis going? Who was it on? Dostoyevski? You've always been very strange. And I still haven't let you talk. Go on. Tèbia will be here in half an hour, and I'd like to have this over with. Go ahead, talk.

HE SPENT THE FIRST TWENTY YEARS OF HIS LIFE IN A CIRCUS, moving from one place to the next, and never, in all those years, did he set foot more than once in the same city. Had there ever been another circus so bent on aimless wandering? The son of acrobats, as an infant he was constantly regaled with new surroundings, and he was a friend to midgets and clowns, tamers and lions, ponies, trapeze artists, tightrope walkers, human cannonballs, and elephants. He came to know three Buffalo Bills and two Indian ballerinas willing to be silhouetted with knives. At the age of 14, he fell in love with a teenage girl who sat in the second row three days straight. The third day (while he was assisting the lady with the trained dogs), the girl winked at him and he blushed. He didn't know how to react, and by the time he had figured out a way to approach her, it was too late: They were already on the road, a train of circus wagons heading for the next city.

When he was twenty, the circus folded. Everyone gave the same old reason: too much competition from the movies and television. Those who could joined other circuses, but not everyone was so fortunate. At his age, he could have found another job (thus emulating not only his parents, but some of the world's finest acrobats), but he decided to have a shot at sedentary existence and see if there was really anything to it.

He became a clerk in the office of a railway company, and in the next twenty years he never once left the city he had chosen, each day deciding upon, revising, and correcting the schedules of the trains, never once feeling homesick for the cities printed on the tickets. He, who had traveled half the world before he was twenty, spent twenty more years shut up in a silent house and an ironclad office to which he walked every morning down the same road. The first few evenings, bored behind closed doors, he remembered all the towns he had visited in a past which each day grew more and more distant. He thought that perhaps one had to acquire a taste for the sedentary existence in a sedentary way: Maybe all he needed was time to get used to it. He soon lost not only the ability to react to the routine that was eating away at him but, even worse, he lost the ability to reminisce during the day. Instead, every night, with the precision of a craftsman, he dreamed a parallel life that was nothing more than the repetition of the first twenty years of his life. In this way (dreaming each night a day from twenty years before), at the age of forty he dreamed that the circus folded and he chose a sedentary existence. He awakened from the nightmare in a sweat and breathing heavily, as if the roof were about to fall in on him. Awake from a twenty-year dream, he sold everything he owned. At the station, he took the first train that came through.

He went from country to country. From the very start, he decided to make up for lost time: He ruled out all of the places he had been as a young man, determined never to set foot in a city he had already seen. About ten years later, half a century old, he had covered half of the half of the world he had not visited in his youth. Every time he took leave of a city, he knew it was forever. Each first glimpse of his surroundings was also his last.

Ten years later, he had toured the entire planet and realized that it was no longer possible to set foot in a land he had never visited. As he hadn't been dreaming for quite some time, he tried to remember the city in which he had first kissed a girl—his cousin from the high-wire act. He wasn't sure if it had been in Berlin or Danzig; he wondered if he had seen everything in sufficient detail. If so, then there was no excuse for such a glaring doubt. Then he realized that many places were hard for him to recall; some parts of the past were fading, and it seemed to him that certain rivers followed a course different from the one he knew to be accurate. He wondered what had been the point of seeing the world only to lose his memory.

Now he felt his life was a tensed coil. Waiting for the train that was to take him to Parma (the first in his long inventory of cities; the one he least remembered, precisely because he had been born there), he realized that it was harder and harder for him to remember what his mother had looked like; it now seemed to him that her image was traced on a liquid mirror, dissolving with the movement of the water. Sitting on the wooden bench, he looked at the weeds between the tracks. He looked at them, but suddenly he didn't understand what he was seeing: their name and those of all other herbs had fled from his memory. He asked himself what that row of small green sprouts was. He felt he was getting lost. He lifted his eyes: On a wall on the other side of the tracks, an enormous circus poster, torn, made him feel happy. He thought going to the circus might not be a bad idea, after so many years away from the big top. When he glanced back at the poster to check the date and place, he was mystified by the white-painted face with a cross on one eye and a vertical line down the other, a hat like a shiny cone, an exaggerated nose and a mouth that laughed twice.

The platform was deserted. He lowered his body until his neck rested on the back of the bench. He closed his eyes. He yawned. He looked right and left. He thought, *if I can't even conjure up the city where I was born* ... He heard a door opening: A woman stuck her head out, looked in both directions, then disappeared.

When he heard the door slam shut, he could no longer remember if it had ever been open, nor who had gone in, nor if anyone had gone in, nor the door.

He hardly had time to ask himself what was happening to him. He remembered (the scene filled his brain so vividly that he couldn't tell whether he was really seeing it or not) a gray pond, under a white sky, by a humid green jungle. Then (and it was obvious he could no longer control these images, which shot off like balloons losing air), a dry hotel tasting of dust, with white walls and wooden Cubist furniture. Suddenly, the images disappeared. He didn't remember a thing. A black rectangle was all that was left; he forgot the name of the city he was going to, he looked in bewilderment at the station, unable to think where it was, or what those parallel lines of steel disappearing on both horizons were there for. When the train arrived, he didn't recognize it. It didn't seem like a machine or a monster, because neither of those words meant anything to him. Since he had also forgotten what it was to be afraid, he didn't run away.

NORTH OF SOUTH

N TOOK THE STAIRS TWO AT A TIME, NERVOUS, FLUSTERED, trying to ignore the beating of his heart. On the last flight of stairs he tried to calm down, and then realized that, in fact, the only outward sign that could make him appear strange was his overly agitated breathing. He took several deep breaths and opened the door, in fear. For a moment, he listened to the silence and tried to extract some information from it. He knew that everything was about to fall apart, to turn into a pile of rubble, and that there was no way to avoid it. Now was not the time, though, to feel sorry and talk about what could have been done and wasn't, because in the moment of truth you just swallow hard, throw caution to the winds, and plow on through. After all is said and done, you only live once or twice. So if the roof and floor cracked and the whole foundation on which he had based his existence for so many years had fallen to pieces, it was simply the least he could have expected of a situation like that, a blind alley that threatened to suck him in forever more and make him disappear down the eye of the endless spiral. He sat down. He let his head roll back.

He imagined S's fury, tense and gaping; staring straight at him as if she didn't recognize him and were only now seeing for the very first time this snake coughing discreetly before her, eyes slinking away from the glare that burned his skin and froze his spine. He found it impossible to envision any other reaction. Then the prospects for the future began to explode about him, becoming uncontrollable. N knew that from that day forward it was the end of the shared candies, the Sunday morning jam, the evening stroll, the kisses in the elevator, the laughter at the race-track, the two tickets to the movies hidden under a hat or a napkin. On the contrary, this was the beginning of chill mornings, Nordic alarm clocks, devastating afternoons of a lion shut up in a cage too big for him, a monk in a cell, a moth-eaten stuffed bird collecting dust.

Clearly, though, eventually the frost would melt, and the Thursday soccer games would begin, the Saturday night card games, the beer cans under the bed, the feet on the table, the breakfasting on champagne before heading off to bed. And not just that; it would also mean the end—forever more—of the visits from all those wrinkled relatives and know-it-all friends who sprinkle the parquet with ashes during de rigueur suppers. And it was the end of stockings on the sofa, unsought advice, hair in the sink, overwrought demands. For a while, N paced up and down the apartment. Then he felt dizzy, wanting to vomit and to eat at the same time. He bathed, straightened books, fussed about resetting the speed on the stereo turntable.

He heard S's steps. She came up the stairs quickly, inserted the key in the lock, opened the door. Like a child closing his eyes so as not to be seen, he didn't look at her and only heard her throw her hat and coat on a chair, say hello, and stare at him with a strength that didn't pierce him—a much weaker glare than he had imagined. Disquieted, N raised his eyes and confronted hers, then realized that she was flustered and trying to control her agitated breathing. N was disconcerted. He thought he had ferreted out all the traps that could befall him, but he had not foreseen this respite. It was more than evident that neither of them had the slightest intention of discussing it, precisely because both of them knew perfectly well what was happening. N realized he had seen the end—before they ever began—of the poker games, the feet up on the table, the Thursday soccer, the beer cans under the bed, the breakfasting on champagne before falling into bed. Of course, he was also seeing the return of the shared candies, the Sunday morning jam, the two tickets hidden under the hat. But that also meant the hair in the sink, the stockings on the sofa, the unsought advice, the visits to all the wrinkled relatives, the know-it-all friends sprinkling the parquet with ashes in formal suppers, the overwrought demands, the all-too-frequent hand wrapped around the knife. He got up (it was clear to him that everything that had run through his head had also run through hers), they pressed their cheeks together, they said hello again, and they kissed each other on the lips, wrapped in a furious embrace.

RINGS

THE MORNING LOOKED LIKE AN EGG. ON THE TENNIS COURT, Enric abandoned himself to his usual acrobatics. For example, his smash was a touch long (or short, or perfect), and Natxo lost the ball (as he often did), which bounced against a wall (or the cyclone fence, or the trees) and rolled to a stop where it fell asleep at the foot of an empty director's chair. Let's assume (to keep it short) that with that ball he pocketed game, set, and match. These are mere details; Enric nearly always won.

Then he showered and dressed. Natxo suggested they have lunch together. Enric said no; he had to meet up with Pepa. They agreed to phone each other about dinner.

Pepa was late. She opened the door of the restaurant, spilling over with apologies. What's more, she had already eaten; a sandwich with the people at school. She was really sorry. Enric thought that a sandwich wasn't really a proper lunch. Pepa said she just wanted a drink. The waiter took the order. Pepa smiled. Enric told her he had bought a summer house on Minorca (for week-ends) and, to make things easier, he was thinking of studying for a small-aircraft pilot's license. Pepa suggested they see a movie.

Two hours later, they were on their way out. They went to Enric's house and got into bed. When the telephone rang at eight o'clock they were half-asleep. It was Natxo, all worked up: He had dialed the wrong number twice in a row and had got the same house twice. They made dinner arrangements. In the bedroom Pepa was still asleep. Enric nibbled at her thighs: "Would you like us to take a shower together?"

Half soaped up, the phone rang again. With a soapy erection, Enric walked about leaving footprints on the tile floor. Pepa touched one of her nipples and looked pissed.

"Yes?"

On the other end there was silence, except for someone breathing.

"Yes?"

The breathing hesitated. It seemed to want to laugh. Enric imagined an apple tree with no apples or leaves, made of card-board; or a mute parrot calling from another world close by. Finally a girl spoke: "Hi, Enric. Don't you remember me?"

Enric didn't remember her. For a moment he thought, "It could be Eva . . . or maybe Anna." He ran through all the possibilities, but the voice was definitely strange to him. His erection had disappeared and droplets of soap were falling to the ground, forming a puddle.

"Well . . ."

"You mean you don't remember a-a-all the things we've done together?"

The voice wanted to be enticing and was laughable. No one can ask "you mean you don't remember all the things we've done together?" except as a joke. When he was about to answer, the voice spoke once again: "I certainly remember you. Do you know what I do when I remember you?" The girl exaggerated her breathing, and clicked her tongue against her palate. "Can you imagine? First I lick one of my fingers, and I suck on it as if it were made of honey. Then, little by little—'cause I'm in no hurry, I have all the time in the world—I run my hand down

my body, caressing it all the way down, each little fold, because it's a fragile body, and deserves great care. And right here
where I'm touching myself, on this little button that quivers, I
die of pleasure, and one of the fingers from my other hand I
stick into a hole, silky and moist . . . just as I am doing now.
Warm and juicy—"

Enric hung up. He tried to guess—for he was certain that he
didn't know the owner of that voice—which of his acquain-
tances, having put the girl up to carrying out her seduction scene,
was now exploding with laughter not two yards away from the
other phone. He saw that his erection was back. He hurried back
and jumped into the shower, splashing water all over the floor.

"Hey!"

"You know who that was? An obscene caller."

"What did the person say?"

"She said she was sticking two fingers into her vagina, just
like this . . ."

"Oops."

When, half a minute later, the telephone rang again, they had
three in—fingers, that is. They played deaf and the ringing went
on and on, like an emergency siren.

The following day, after he won the match, Enric had lunch
with a bank officer. Later, Lídia called. He arranged to pick her
up that evening.

At home, Enric changed, listened to music, read a report and,
at eight o'clock sharp, when the telephone rang, he was yawn-
ing over *International Management*.

"Hi, Enric. You still don't remember me?"

" . . ."

"You know, last night I was thinking about you for the long-
est time and—"

"And you stuck three fingers in your vagina?"

"Four. 'Cause I was nice and wet and they went in so smoothly,
like never before—"

Enric hung up. The last thing he needed was to consent to
pranks. He got dressed. He put Klaus Schulze (Lídia's favorite

kind of music) on the record player and left it ready to flip
on as soon as they got home.

For three days the call came, always at the same time. The
fourth evening, Enric gathered a group of his friends—both
men and women, all of whom were in on the story—by the telephone. Every time the phone rang, a different person picked
up the receiver and declared it to be a wrong number. The fifth
time, the voice cried out "you idiot."

That night, Enric went to bed earlier than usual. The following morning, for the first time in six months, he lost a game.
Annoyed, he didn't call Pepa, as arranged, and he squandered
the afternoon on foolish purchases and an antique vase. At two
minutes to eight the phone rang. This surprised him, for the anonymous caller was scrupulously punctual. He picked up the receiver. It was Pepa: So what was going on? At fifteen seconds to
eight, Enric made an excuse; he'd call her back later. The minute he put the receiver down, the telephone rang again.

"Yes?"

"Hi . . ."

(From this point on the story is easy to imagine and, as a re-
sult, perhaps more tiresome. We will therefore be brief, avoid-
ing, on the one hand, psychological explanations—wild cards always
on hand to justify any deed—and, on the other, the descrip-
tion of his friends' reactions; the growing concern of the board
at the bank; and the measures taken by his family, who were
by turns amazed, distraught, indignant and resolute. All very pre-
dictable and progressively more serious.)

For days, Enric tried to make a date with the mysterious
voice. After many evenings of siege, the voice finally agreed: Tomorrow, at eight, at a stipulated place. Enric described himself
so she would recognize him—gray suit and red carnation in the
buttonhole. The voice found this cute. Enric was glad.

The following evening at eight, for the first time in weeks, he
was not by the telephone. The meeting place was full of people, and no one came up to him. There was, of course, no way
of knowing if she was there or not, and if she was, who she

was. He went home late and plastered, with keys far too big for such small locks. The next time she called, he was indignant. The voice said she had been there, at the appointed time and place, but that she had preferred not to say anything, and simply to observe his reactions. Angry, Enric hung up the phone and, even as he put it down, was already regretting it, for he realized that she didn't want to play any more. He sat by the phone waiting for it to ring, but it didn't. He slept poorly, and the next evening at eight the telephone remained mute. When it finally did ring again, three days later, it was only to tell him that the game was over, that she had had enough of this schoolgirl prank that had only begun, by chance, one evening when someone had dialed her number twice asking for a certain Enric and repeating the correct number, of which she had made note. That had been enough to start things rolling. But now she wouldn't be calling any more. Enric asked for a meeting. She said it wasn't worth their while. He persisted. She roundly refused. He was afraid she would hang up and decided not to insist on meeting her, instead suggesting the game go on as before—one call a day. But she said that her mind was made up; she would not be calling again. She hung up.

Enric considered the possibilities. If she had learned his name and number from a couple of misdialings, then their phone numbers must be quite similar; perhaps one or two digits apart, no more. He decided to try out all the possible numerical combinations. In a few days, his finger was tired and fear grew in him that perhaps her number was one of the many that rang on indefinitely, answered by no one. He went on with this for weeks, dialing thousands of numbers. To no avail.

He imagined a hundred thousand possible deaths. Every evening, when he hung up the phone after an exhausting day of dialing—until eight, just in case—he decided upon a different suicide. He went so far as to compose a most extensive handbook. He imagined the last scene of the film, always the same: eight o'clock, just as they carried his body off inside the casket, the telephone would ring, one day too late.

Everything turned out quite differently, however. After weeks of plumbing the deepest abysses of ignominy, barricaded in the darkest corner of the house (evading police investigations, end-less brigades of psychoanalysts sent by his family, the onslaught of his friends), one night under his front door he found a note from the telephone company dated quite a while back, with the imminent threat (therefore, already in effect) of cutting off his line. He ran to the phone and picked up the receiver, al-ready knowing what he would find: The line was dead. He then realized that at some point in his family's effort to cut off all his bank accounts (in the face of the evidence of his considerable madness), a mistake must have been made and even his auto-matic payment services had been canceled.

The end of the story is lost, now, through labyrinths, down corridors to windows of a Plateresque bureaucracy, all in an attempt to pay his bills and reconnect his phone, in the ever slim-mer hope that the calls would resume, finally taking advantage of one of these sorties out onto the street to call, at first with some chagrin, Lídia (or maybe Pepa), from a telephone booth: "Hi, babe."

"My God! Are you finally out of quarantine?"

RUSSIAN DOLLS

HE RUNS THROUGH THE FIELDS, HIDING AMONG THE TALL GRASSES, behind the columns. The house lies farther and farther behind. To the right of the road are riverbank trees and every so often a white wooden sign with black letters: BADEN VERBOTEN. At the end of the numerous short paths, perpendicular to the main road, there are staircases that sink into the lake with balustrades adorned with stone vases and flowers. He pants. He sweats. He's very tired. He leans on one of the balustrades. He alternately looks behind him and toward the water, nervously. Now he is walking along the lake down to the dock, which is deserted. He surveys the horizon. He knows that if they take much longer, he's a goner. He goes back up the stairs. He jumps over the balustrade. He hides among the trees. From there he can see the lake. He feels impatient. He looks at his watch constantly. Soon he hears a faint sound that grows continually louder. In the distance, between the livid blues of the sky and the water, a boat

with an outboard motor appears. A bird cuts through the air.
He gets up from the ground. He carefully separates the branches,
looks toward the road, jumps the balustrade. As he goes down
the stone staircase leading to the dock he hears a noise behind
him. He turns his head. The brunette with dark glasses is pointing a pistol at him. The music gets louder. He begins to run
toward the water. . . .

The screen goes black, then white. The people whistle. A few
of them shout. The lights go on. For a moment, the noise di-
minishes. Then, ten slow minutes go by during which the audience slips from waiting more or less patiently to waiting in
annoyance: They stamp their feet and demand an explanation. Confusion breaks out when, finally, a representative of the theater
comes out to apologize, flustered, and explains that something
unheard-of has occurred: The end of the picture is gone. And
it doesn't seem, he adds, that anyone has made off with it, since,
after the last frames they saw, and without a break in rhythm,
there's a long length of blank film. He is very sorry for their
trouble, above all because he is aware that at a premiere this
kind of mix-up is particularly annoying. He apologizes, more-
over and emphatically, to the press, and concludes by saying
that, under the circumstances, the only thing he can do is to re-
fund the price of the tickets, to which end the public is re-
quested to leave the theater in an orderly manner and line up at
the box office. Contact has been made with the distributors, he
goes on, who profess their ignorance in the matter and promise
to initiate inquiries with the producers. The man finally waves
his arms in a gesture of impotence and goes off. After a wave of
protests, the audience slowly files out. The spectator (one among
the multitude—any one) yawns, gets up with an effort, moves
toward the lobby. The line of people waiting for their refunds
at the box office blends in with the line of people waiting to get
in for the next show who, now perplexed, are unwilling to aban-
don the privileged place they have achieved for themselves in
the line by dint of their considerable wait. Our man doesn't feel
like waiting. He gives his money up for lost and takes off up
the street. Halfway down the line of those waiting to get in he
hears a travesty of the story being passed along: They are saying

that someone has seized the film in order to get publicity for a movie project that no production company has been willing to finance. By the tail end of the line, the story has been totally transformed. They are saying that someone has phoned the movie house warning of a bomb. People scatter through the side streets, discreetly alarmed. He gets into his car and takes off. Dizzy Gillespie is on the radio. He drives down outlying streets, white and opaque. Now a reporter on the radio is interviewing a woman with no arms who has given birth to a child with no legs. The announcer thereby concludes, in something of a dither, that one thing leads to another and switches right back to Dizzy: "Russian Lullaby," a song the man also hears (to his surprise) coming from the Muzak in the restaurant. At the table, he orders a gastronomic palindrome (first course—melon with prosciutto; second course—fresh ham; dessert—melon) in the hope of astonishing the maître d', who seems ill-disposed to having his composure ruffled so easily. At a nearby table, someone is speaking of an Australian telepathist who awakened, terrified, from a dream at the exact moment that a Swiss colleague was being subjected to a terrible shock caused by a mischievous niece who had taken to wearing outlandish costumes. Our man laughs, and his laughter increases throughout the meal until, by dessert time, he is reduced to a cascade of bells and tympanies resounding through all the dungeons of the castle. . . .

The alarm clock. Dragging himself about listlessly, he showers, shaves, dresses. He has breakfast at the bar across the street. Then he gets into his car. He leaves the city behind and for ten minutes the highway is deserted. He sees the house off in the distance. He parks close by. To the right of the road, riverbank trees. By the side of the lake, lights, cables and circuit panels. They had been waiting for him for quite some time. He changes in seconds. They make him up. The director gives the order to start shooting. He hides among the trees. They shoot from several angles. Then he jumps the balustrade. He repeats the jump twice. As he goes down the stone staircase, he hears a sound behind him; he turns his head. The brunette with dark glasses is pointing a pistol at him. He begins running toward the water. They repeat the scene. Twice in a row the girl takes aim and he breaks into a sprint. The director is still not satisfied. They repeat it a third time. The girl points a pistol at him, he begins to run toward the water. The director doesn't interrupt the shooting. The girl fires, the actor falls to the ground.

In the loge, there is a moment of consternation: someone in the audience has fallen to the floor. They carry him off just as the film comes to an end.

TO CHOOSE

When a man cannot choose he ceases to be a man.... Is a man who chooses the bad perhaps in some way better than a man who has the good imposed upon him?
                    —Anthony Burgess, *A Clockwork Orange*

BY MIDMORNING, HAVING CLEARED UP MY CORRESPONDENCE AND preparing to look over some drafts, I felt a kind of void in my stomach. It was definitely not hunger. This was a palpable emptiness, like a ball I couldn't quite digest. If I could have stuck my hand down my throat, I would have been able to touch it, soft and greasy, a nothingness that complained in silence. Downstairs, on the main floor, I had coffee. A half hour later, my uneasiness persisted. This time I had a glass of mineral water in the bar across the street. I waited another quarter of an hour; now it was as if my insides were full of air. If someone had pricked me, I would have burst. I asked to speak with my boss and told him I didn't feel well and I was requesting his permission to go home. I described the malady in some confusion: It was my stomach, and it was getting increasingly worse. I capped it off with a bad headache, just in case the symptoms seemed unsubstantial to him. He gave me permission to go home and wished me a rapid recovery.

On the way home, I meditated. A kind of odd anguish began creeping up my spine, without my realizing that it was metamorphosing into a desire it would be impossible for me to control. Toward midafternoon, I began simultaneously to understand what was happening and to resist accepting the fact. To keep this obsession at bay, I busied myself fixing plugs, hanging light fixtures, clearing bookshelves. In that one afternoon I dispensed with all the chores I had been putting off for months.

That evening, as I watched TV, I managed to formulate the thing in a coherent fashion. Then, as if hoping that on hearing the words, clear and round, fear would steer me away from such roiling paths, I said it aloud:

"I must kill someone."

Thus articulated—in all its coldness—the effect was the opposite of what I had hoped. It was as if the signifiers made the signified less grave (*vous pigez la feinte?*). Naturally, I formulated the appropriate objections: It was a dangerous, gratuitous, amoral escapade. Usually, when a man thinks of killing someone, it is precisely *someone* that he wants to kill, and for more or less concrete motives. I, on the other hand, found myself at a far remove from such simple sentiments. I felt the need to kill, with no motive. And this need, far from causing me any distress, would, if carried to its logical end, leave me feeling free, joyful, and alive.

I didn't sleep well that night. Bad dreams assailed me, but not because I was on the verge (On the verge? Was it all so clear, even in the dream?) of committing a (shall we say) heinous crime, but rather because I was taking too long to make my decision. At one point in the dream—somewhere between a desert of cornstalks and a building with no doors—I comprehended a truth so true that it seemed atrocious to me: He who commits a crime is not guilty but he who, having committed a crime, lets himself be caught, is. The next morning, in a sweat, I called the office claiming a galloping case of flu. My boss recommended aspirin, cognac, warm milk, honey and lemon, and bed rest.

While breakfasting on fruit juice, I did some lengthy woolgathering: Whom would I kill, and why? It crossed my mind—I had heard it said, I don't know where—that the perfect crime can only take place when it is impossible to establish any connection whatsoever between the criminal and the victim. If I killed an anonymous passerby without anyone seeing me, how could they suspect me, if even I didn't know who it was? I would be like a sniper who shoots at people he doesn't know, the difference being that I would avoid the exhibitionism that so often leads to their being caught.

Therefore, it was not necessary for me to decide whom I should kill; pure chance would lead me to my victim. On some lonely corner, without even looking at his face, I would kill someone, and not till the following day in the newspapers would I see his face and learn his name. The only thing to premeditate was the instrument. Right from the start I ruled out cars. To crush someone at a hundred per in a dark alley seemed to befit a clumsy apprentice—and traceable. Knives seemed brutish to me. The stocking around the neck, sordid. More than anything else, the revolver was my speed: It would turn me into a letter-perfect assassin.

What's more, I would dress appropriately. I designed my wardrobe: pinstripe suit (with vest), dark shirt, light tie, dress shoes. I spent less time in dressing and taking up arms than I might have expected. I resurrected some shoes with laces—real beauties—from the top shelf of a closet. At the arms supplier I ran into no difficulties. The outrageous ease of obtaining a weapon for personal defense made personal attack easier than ever. That very afternoon everything was ready. I slept the whole night through.

The next morning the mirror showed me a face that was anything but criminal. After so many years of mutual companionship, I can admit that my face—a bit too pale, slack in the jaw, and not at all aggressive—resembles something halfway between a fish and an egg. Before I went out the door—and not

yet fully believing the whole thing—I placed the weapon between my belt and my shirt.

I meandered through a park all morning. I ate lunch at a snack
bar on a square with a fountain in the center. Then I strolled
past a stand of poplars that I had thought long gone. All afternoon I kept running my hand over the handle of the revolver.
By the side of a tinfoil lake an old woman was feeding birdseed
to the pigeons. We were completely alone. I kept walking. Much
farther on, a watchman was sitting on a bench, languidly cleaning his fingernails. I felt no temptation to shoot him. Later,
under some trees, I saw a couple doing more than kissing. They
filled my heart with tenderness.

So picky, who was I to kill? They all seemed too gray to die.
Perhaps some outstanding personality? In some vague way, I
knew that none of the individuals I had seen was the one I was
looking for. Was I, then, looking for someone in particular?
Along the road leading to the park exit, I was approached by a
man. He was neither young nor old, neither tall nor short, and
so ordinary that you could have passed right by him without taking note of his presence. A guy like that was ideal. I took the
revolver out from between my liver and my belt and put it in
my jacket pocket. Ten steps away from him, I placed my finger on the trigger. On the verge of shooting—and I myself was
surprised at how easy it would have been—I saw that, in point
of fact, such a paragon of mediocrity didn't do it for me either.
I went back to my ruminations and, in an attempt to dispel
them, repeated to myself that the proper course was to kill
without motive, because that was the only way to carry out a
crime with impunity. For a moment I saw myself as having no
character. How easy it must be to pull the trigger for a cause!
When I turned my head, the ordinary man was already quite a
ways off.

I had a shot of gin in a bar. I got into the car and headed out
of the city: I chose highways I was familiar with and roads I
wasn't. At a considerable distance from any trace of urban de-
velopment, surrounded by cypresses and under a full moon, I
came across a two-story country house with the lights on. Si-
lently, I parked the car among the trees.

As I ran across the fields, half-crouching, it seemed to me that
I had lived this whole scene before—in a previous incarnation,
or perhaps at the movies. Now I was right by the front door. I
could see inside through a window. In a spacious living room,
with walls overcrowded with paintings, a man about forty years
old was watching TV. Was anyone else home? The man took
a cigar from a wooden box. I heard a noise. Upstairs the lights
had gone out and a woman was now outlined in the doorway
to the living room wearing a heavy fur overcoat. The man and
the woman kissed. I could hear snatches of their conversation.
He urged her to come home early. She promised to return as
soon as the movie was over. I hid behind some plants, but instead of coming out the door she went directly to the garage,
emerging in a white Mercedes at high speed.

I decided the old story about wanting to use the phone because the car broke down would be less plausible than inventing a situation in a way that would arouse the man's concern.
(Since, given the circumstances, it would be easy.) I waited several minutes, during which time the man cut the tip off his cigar and lighted it with care. Then I knocked impetuously:

"Open up! Your wife has had an accident!"

I could only hear the voices on the television. (Now, at the
front door, I couldn't see inside.) Then I heard the TV being
turned off and footsteps, but I couldn't figure out if they were
coming or going. I felt the revolver, still in my pocket. I
repeated:

"Open up! There's been an accident. Your wife ... in a white
Mercedes ... !"

The man undid the latch and opened the door slowly, disconcerted. But I must not have seemed malevolent, for upon seeing
me he opened the door wider, trusting, and said:

"My wife? I'm not married. But the white Mercedes ..."

It had been my mistake; I had jumped to a conclusion. The
woman who had left was therefore not his wife. So what? He
should have understood me. Perhaps it was his lover, a girlfriend
I suddenly felt sorry for. It hadn't even occurred to him that it
might be she until he heard me mention the white Mercedes. By
now I was inside the house and the silence had been thicken-

ing for too long. This was definitely my man. I took out the revolver. The man made a gesture of surprise. I felt obliged to
say a word or two to clear up the situation:

"I've come to kill you."

The man now looked even more surprised. It was evident that,
when he saw the weapon, he had imagined I had come to rob
him. With a thin voice, he asked me why. I wasn't going to go
along with that game. If I began to explain that, in fact, I had
no reason to liquidate him, I would soon feel out of place, ab-
surd. The man then said:

"Just a moment. I'll give you anything you want." He took
off his watch—which was gold—and handed it to me with his
wallet. "I have jewels upstairs, and more cash. If you wish, you
can have these paintings. You could get a lot for them. But
don't get nervous ... let's not get nervous."

He was rapidly becoming terrified. He didn't want to believe
that I wasn't there to rob him. He was incapable of understanding the situation. I was offended at his taking me for a com-
mon thief, easily bought off with a couple of baubles. Trembling
and stuttering, he seemed so cowardly to me (and as I felt the cold
of the trigger on my fingertip it occurred to me that in his place
I would have behaved with similar cowardice) that I didn't feel
the slightest remorse as I let go two shots, which resounded in
the night like smacks in the face. I finished him off on the floor
with a third shot. The cigar began to burn a corner of the carpet. The man still grasped the wallet and watch he had offered
me. I bent down. Not entirely understanding what I was doing,
I took the watch and the wallet. Upstairs, I gathered up the jewels and the cash. I selected five of the paintings: a Modigliani,
two Bacons, a Hopper and a Llimós. I used my handkerchief to
turn the knob. In the car, as I drove off, I asked myself whether
the next time it would be as easy to set things up as it had
been this time.

THE LETTER

WEDNESDAY NOON HE SHUT ALL THE DOORS AND WINDOWS TO the kitchen, turned on the gas, stretched out on the floor, belly up, and died a short time later. Friday morning, before the people from the funeral parlor arrived, the mailman brought a letter in an envelope with no return address. (A distant cousin, the only relative they could come up with, had already left some time before, alleging unavoidable duties and such a tenuous kinship that he had been able to accomplish the necessary grieving in one night's vigil, particularly in light of his staunch agnosticism.) The doorman took the letter and, not knowing what else to do with it, left it on the corpse's chest. The people from the funeral parlor arrived late and in a hurry. They closed the coffin and took it downstairs. The doorman closed the door to the apartment. The letter, which no one read, said:

Dear asshole,
   Your letters have been coming for a few weeks now, but I haven't had time to read them till a couple of days ago.

And I haven't had a moment to answer until now. Understand that this is the first and last time you'll be hearing from me. It's not my job, you know, to spend my time and energy consoling weaklings like you. You're trying to fill my head with unasked-for promises and proposals that are totally out of place. You're really out of it, man. You know very well I'll never go back to you. We got everything there was to get out of our time together and it wasn't much to speak of, either. So don't come to me now with your sob stories! Have a little character. You say that I went off with Bert because the sex was better with him than with you and you say it as if it were an insult meant to make me feel like a tramp. You're quite mistaken if you think you're going to make me feel bad. Who do you think you are? As a matter of fact, you're absolutely right when you say I have a better time with Bert. You bet I do! I wish you could understand the distance between you two—and I'm also referring to the mental distance. And since you're a bit of a masochist, I'll tell you that just by whispering in my ear all the things he's planning to do to me, he makes me go all wet in a way you never did. I feel like honey and cream melting on the fire. I could spend hours and hours caressing him, making him come whenever and wherever I please. And then I need only start over again ... he's so different from you! He has something called imagination. I don't know if you'd know what that is ... in a restaurant, halfway through dinner, he'll make me take my panties off, and things like that, which you'd consider out of place (what's the point of taking off your panties in a restaurant, you're saying), and he drives me wild, so wild we have to flee from the restaurant as fast as we can. We cling to each other on the street, like two kids. And we sneak into people's yards and roll in the grass, excited just to think that someone could come upon us at any moment. Then we get into a cab and he touches me in such a way that I have to hide my face and bite my hand so as not to cry out with pleasure, and act as if nothing were going on so the cabdriver won't notice; and Bert all serious as if his hand

weren't his, and I come over and over again until we leave
the seat soaking wet and laugh when we get out just to
think of the expression on the next passenger's face. Do you
like my telling you these things? Sure you do. You must
be having a ball, suffering . . . you've always liked suffering
and torturing yourself for nothing. Maybe you're getting
all excited reading about how Bert touches me. He kneads
me and he feels me up and he sticks his fingers everywhere, in all the holes he can find, and I do the same to
him. We make love in parks and movie houses and mo-
tels, as if we couldn't wait to get home. And when we do get
home, we start all over! And I fondle him all around and
play with him anywhere: in the street, in bars, in front of
his friends and mine, in the car while he's driving. On
the bus, when it's full, I stick my hand inside his coat, inside his pants, and I grab on to it, hard, firm, and hot
and I move my hand up and down in time with the jolting
of the bus until he paints my fingers white and I lick them
as we get off and the passenger next to the door sees my
lips and fingers and figures out what's going on and grins
in surprise. You can jerk off, if you like. If, on the other
hand, it hurts you to read all this, you know what to do:
Don't ever write me again. If you were normal, by now—
almost two months after we split up—you'd have a girlfriend
and you'd be fooling around with her instead of trying to
make me feel guilty with your silly letters. If it's any
consolation—or maybe just to make you suffer a little more—
you should know that I've started going out with a real
cute guy, and Bert's a little jealous, just like you the first
time I told you I was going out with Bert. I really have a
great time with this kid. Maybe even better than with Bert,
which isn't easy, and which probably confirms your theory that whenever I pick up a new boyfriend I get all wound
up and everything seems better than later on when I begin to know him better and lose interest. Maybe it's true—
but so what? This one's real young and I have to teach
him everything: how to use his body, what to do to me, how
to lick me, how to hold me. I feel protective, like a mother.

It must be my maternal instinct coming out, or something. He's gentle and strong as a calf and he fills my mouth with a sweetness I've never tasted before. It must be his age ... his soft, boyish touch. Do you still want more news of me? I hope not. And as far as your suicide threat is concerned, I find it in bad taste and not at all original, because if you mean to pressure me like Tony did when I left him to go and live with you, I must remind you that he, at least, had the guts to do it, which, in your case, I find a little doubtful. Well, then, dear heart, truly hoping never to hear from you again, and with my most lukewarm regards,

C.

FOUR QUARTERS

THE DICTIONARY SAYS PUNCTUAL MEANS ON TIME, WHICH MAY
be taken to mean that if you arrange to meet at seven, you
are a punctual person if you show up at seven. Quite clear,
thus far. What seems less clear is how to define a person who,
having agreed to meet at seven, is already roaming the streets in
the vicinity of the meeting place at six, and by six-thirty has
come to a stop next to the newsstand, which is the meeting place
mainly because it's Friday. On Friday newsstands blossom like
gardens in spring, since all the weekend periodicals appear at once,
and there are few things in this world more entertaining while
waiting than slowly perusing the covers of magazines (and books,
on display in the racks on the side). At six forty-five, though,
all covers have been more than seen and, since a quarter of an
hour still lies ahead, a magazine or a newspaper for leisurely
leafing through is in order. Having read the last line of the last
column of the last page (the only one that begs to be read: the

entertainment page), it's now seven o'clock and there's no reasonable excuse for feeling tired of waiting since in fact the *real*
waiting period has not yet begun. The said individual, at once
punctual (in the right place at exactly the assigned moment) and
not punctual (in the right place ahead of time, therefore not exactly at the assigned moment) in this case, is I: ever in a quan-
dary as to how to define this exacerbated nonpunctual punctuality
that has plagued me since childhood, to my dismay and to the
amazement of the people with whom I make appointments, who
are ordinarily obsessively tardy. Being tardy may mean making
a date for seven and showing up at one minute past seven or at
five past seven or at a quarter past seven or at half-past seven
or at nine or at ten. (The fact that many people arrive late because they enjoy having people wait for them is so obvious as
to require no further comment.) And he (or she) who, in the end,
does not show up for an appointment at all, automatically ceases
to be considered tardy, deserving of being called a swine. If, with
luck, you know the person you're waiting for, you may classify
him or her in the proper category, and even go so far as to for-
give the delay (or be surprised at an unaccustomed punctuality,
or worry over an accident that has not taken place). If you do
not know him or her (or, at very least, are unfamiliar with his
or her habits as regards appointments), risk and adventure stalk
your immediate future. In all likelihood, you will spend a great
deal of time as an imperturbable mannequin leaning against
walls and lampposts, dreaming up delightful acts of vengeance
and classifying, by way of distraction, all the various and sun-
dry types of punctual and nonpunctual beings with whom the
fates confront us throughout life.

   This last-cited case above was mine: I was totally ignorant of
the social habits of the girl I was waiting for (I had always
met her before on the way out of the nuclear plant where we both
work—that's how I know her). So, by quarter past seven I had
looked at all the covers and read not one but two periodicals (to
be precise: one newspaper and one magazine). At half past, I
began to wonder if perhaps we had arranged to meet somewhere else; or at another time; or if she had understood it was
to be at another place or time; or if I was the one who had mis-

understood; or if something had happened to her; or if she had
backed out and decided not to come (when I had vacuumed the
whole carpet and stocked champagne in the refrigerator, in prep-
aration for a mad evening!); or if the traffic was chaotic in some
part of the city (I remembered, though, that she didn't have a
car, so vehicular chaos wouldn't affect her); or if what was
malfunctioning was the subway (a crash; a derailment; cadavers on the platform—maybe hers?); or if something else had im-
peded her coming (her mother hit by a car; her father lost down
an elevator shaft; her little brother—did she have any brothers,
younger or older?—arrested for trafficking in marbles). At nine,
I began to consider the possibility of giving up. At quarter past
nine they closed the newsstand (and the vendor looked at me
as if I were a ghost—or a thief—as he pulled down the iron gate).
I thought it would be a good idea to have a coffee in the bar
next to the newsstand. At half-past, I went in, and the warmth
made me realize that outside in the street it was cold as hell.
And I'd been out there for three hours! I stayed at the bar (since
hope, they say, springs eternal) because from there I could keep
an eye on the street and the newsstand just in case she appeared, breaking the national record for lateness, which is going
some. I asked for a coffee with milk.

At ten o'clock (you must have realized by now that these things
didn't happen, as they usually do not, at each quarter of the
hour on the dot; however, for me to be more precise with re-
gard to the minutes would be irritating), I paid for my coffee
and, when I turned toward the door, I saw Helena sitting there.
(Let us not get all worked up ahead of time: Helena was not
the girl I had been waiting for all evening. The girl I had been
waiting for all that time was Hortènsia. And, by the way, allow me to introduce myself. My name is Hilari.) Helena had been
my girlfriend in college, until the year before. When I finished
my degree, I finished with Helena. We were now kissing each
other's cheeks.

"You've really changed ..."

"Not so much. You look the same to me."

"It's been a year, hasn't it? ... It seems much longer. You look heavier. What are you up to? Where do you work? Tell me about yourself. . . ."

"Sure . . . but . . ."

"Sit down."

"I was just leaving . . ."

"What are you having?"

"I was having a . . ."

"Sit down. It seems weird to see you standing there. Have you grown? You seem taller."

"Don't be ridiculous! How could I be growing at this stage of the game?"

"So what do you want to drink?"

"Uhh . . . a cognac."

I sat down, realizing that I wasn't at all pleased at the prospect of Hortènsia's appearing and finding me with Helena. I wondered if it would be better to leave right then and there. Perhaps Hortènsia was approaching the newsstand at that very moment (a most unlikely prospect; it was clear that she belonged to the genus of the swine), or stay there with Helena and run still another risk (which I now wished were not only improbable, but impossible): of Hortènsia's arriving a little later and coming into the bar and finding us there.

"I saw you come in, a half hour ago."

It didn't occur to me to ask her why she hadn't greeted me. I thought to myself that I hadn't seen her enter (which was very odd, as I had been next to the newsstand all evening). How long had she been there? Had she seen me, a mannequin abandoned next to a newsstand, obviously waiting for someone—someone who had not yet come. (And what about her, was she waiting for someone? Would she ask me if I was? What should I say if she did?)

"Have you been here long?"

Half-baked strategist that I was, I had asked first.

"A good while. It was so cold outside that I came in to have a hot drink."

(What was a "while" to her? What standard did she use to judge whether a while was long or short? And that bit about how cold it was outside . . . was she teasing me?) We fell silent for a few moments, or a moment, or perhaps some fragments of a moment that seemed to me to be very lengthy seconds. It was time to say something. Unforeseeable events—and that encounter was one—shake me, they make me nervous. Something similar must have been happening to her, because I hadn't answered her last question and she didn't seem to notice. We went on casting about for a topic. Suddenly Helena started a serious conversation:

"You know, when we stopped seeing each other, I felt awful. Really awful. Really. We don't have to go over old ground. Both of us know what happened. I ... well, I'm not sure ... we both had something to do with it, right? We decided not to blame each other. Fine. I just want you to know that, at the same time I felt so down, I felt really good, good in an odd way. It was as if I were myself again—and I don't like the expression, it seems facile and cheap. A few days after we broke up, I went to the movies, alone—I don't remember what they were showing—I went to the movies and, when I left, I looked at the floor. It was carpeted in red with great big squares. And it was as if I had always looked at it but was now *seeing* it for the first time, as if I had never seen it before. And, broken up as I was, I felt sure of myself, looking at that carpet and those gray sofas and those black lacquer doors, and I felt like talking with someone, picking up some nice romantic guy, soft and tender. I don't know if I'm making my point. I felt as if the world was there for me, good or bad, and that I was really pretty fucked up. But hell, in any case, it was *I* who was fucked up, *me*. And then when I went outside and saw the cars, the people, I enjoyed thinking that I didn't have to be in a certain place at a certain time to meet up with a certain person and I could, well, have an almond drink or go to see another movie or the same one or sit on a bench and wait for the garbage truck to go by ... or see whomever I pleased, or not see anyone...."

I didn't open my mouth. She stopped talking for a moment, perhaps just to take a breath, because she started right up again:

"This year I've been going out with a guy—Hipòlit—at school—I still haven't graduated. I don't know if you'd remember him. He's a tall redhead with an enormous nose, who played basketball.

We were going out until last week, when we were supposed to get together and he didn't show—"

"You had a date and he broke it?"

"Exactly. The next day he called, with a reasonable excuse. And I believed him, because the excuse—I checked it out right away—was true. Sometimes when these things happen they don't really mean anything, but that day I saw very clearly that everything had been over between Hipòlit and me for a long time, and not because of any foolishness about his not showing up for a date. That was just the catalyst. All at once, I saw the obvious ... that feeling I told you about, of recognizing myself once again in the world around me. Well, I described it with such passion because now I'm beginning to live it all over again, and the red carpet is the one I saw this afternoon at the movies ..."

As Helena spoke, I had been forgiving each and every one of the low blows that she had dealt me in the past. Shall we say I was once again falling reasonably in love with her? I began to doubt if I had ever really hated her that year. She shifted in her seat as if to leave. I suggested getting together. Monday?

"Monday's no good for me."

"Me either, as a matter of fact."

"Tuesday I can't make it."

"It's fine for me, but if it's bad for you ..."

"And Wednesday's out, too."

"How about Thursday? No. Come to think of it, Thursday's out for me. And Friday? Friday's fine with me."

"But not with me. You know what it is? Every time I break up with a boyfriend I fill up the time taking courses. When I broke up with you, I started studying Italian. Now I've started German."

"Listen, I'm not sure ..."

"How about tomorrow? Tomorrow's good for me. If not, we'll have to wait a week."

We made the date. We'd get together the following day—at the same bar, at seven.

At home, I found a message on the answering machine. Hortènsia hadn't been able to come because she had gotten sick a half hour before our date. She was very sorry. When she called—at six—I had already left.

The following day, Saturday, I slept late. I couldn't remember if Helena was punctual or not. Just in case, I decided to play the role of the slightly tardy person, which makes one seem less anxious: I would get to the bar at 7:03. Irritatingly nonpunctual punctual person that I am, at six o'clock I was three blocks over, looking in shop windows. I bought some chestnuts and ate them slowly, looking for garbage cans to throw the shells in. Scandalously punctual with my own decisions, at 7:03 I was standing in front of the bar, shooting a quick glance at the newsstand and at the newsseller (who looked askance at me, as if he felt he had seen me before). In the bar I sat at a table and ordered anisette. The quarters of an hour filed by, one after the other: Helena did not appear. At nine I left: I bought a newspaper at the stand. Next to me, buying another, was Hortènsia, surprised to see me and apologizing for not having shown up the evening before, pointing at the guilty party: her stomach, whose pains had been brought on by an ill-digested lunch. Now, though—and she was very sorry about it—she was in a hurry. We made arrangements for the following day. The following day, I waited only until half-past eight. Hortènsia did not appear. On the corner, I ran into Helena. She was running late. In great haste, she expressed her regret at not having shown up the day before. We set a date for the following day (she'd work things out, she said, to cancel her other commitments). The following day she didn't show. Across the street, however, I ran into Hortènsia, who was hailing the same taxi I was, and which we ended up taking together. She begged my forgiveness and asked if we could get together the next day. The next day I waited in vain and, fed up, started walking home, taking the scenic route through the art galleries. I found Helena standing before a Magritte and she asked ...

I imagined a conspiracy. They were friends and they were getting off on me, and every evening they giggled together, telling each other where and how they had found me, the expression on my face.... I played along with them for a month. Then I had had enough. I made a date with one of them and I didn't

show up. Instead of going to the bar where we'd arranged to
meet, I hid in the one across the street, keeping watch at a distance to see if the one I had not arranged to meet was lurking
somewhere nearby in order to follow me as soon as I left the
bar and run into me *by chance.* I was standing at the bar when
a guy not entirely unfamiliar to me approached. He was a tall
redhead who looked like a basketball player.

"I think I know you," he said formally, calling me by my last
name. Responding with similar formality, I apprised him of my
assumption that he must be Helena's ex-boyfriend. We talked.
He had not kept his date with Helena, a month and a day before, for the same reason that I had not done so that evening. It
was evident that he knew Hortènsia and had been put through the
same routine as I. We began to use first names. We reminisced
about our college days (a year past for me, still current for him).
We decided to have dinner together and throughout the meal
we tried to figure out why they had behaved that way. What
if they weren't acting on their own volition? Perhaps we weren't
the only ones to have been taken in this way and the city was
full of clowns like us. Perhaps it was a worldwide plot: Women
from all over the planet had joined forces in one master ploy
to drive men crazy, before striking the final blow and setting up
a new matriarchy. We ordered a third bottle of champagne. We
must, with all due speed, warn the world of our discovery, or-
ganize men to face the peril. . . . Hipòlit suggested a counterat-
tack. One of us would have to meet an ex-girlfriend of the
other's; the wheel would begin to turn. All men, all over the
world, would make dates with all women and neither one nor
the other would keep their appointments. . . .

In the wee hours, we said good-bye. We arranged to get together the next day, to firm up our strategy: at such-and-such
a time, such-and-such a place. Of course the next day, sober, I
didn't show up.

A MOVIE HOUSE

IT WAS RAINING OUT.

It was a run-down movie house, with peeling paint which, in a season most definitely past, had been cream-colored. The façade was covered with faded posters, bearing the faces of actors who had surely died decades before, made up with glitter and dusty stars. When I entered they were still showing slides. I hadn't had to wait in line and the woman in the box office took care of tearing the tickets in half herself, a cutback in staff that (in case it wasn't otherwise evident) demonstrated that the business was in bad straits.

Although the loge was nearly empty, an usher accompanied me down (unperturbed by the absurdity of being somewhat less than indispensable) limping over the peanut shells, the plastic bags, the Kleenexes, the newspapers, and the condoms that carpeted the floor of the theater. I ought to have left right then, but I didn't. The usher spit on the floor. I chose a seat right on the center aisle, neither very close to nor very far from the screen. The slide show came to an end and, just for a second, the lights went on. On the side walls only a few crimson rags remained of ancient brocades. The darkness returned and the sound of the film projector's motor filled the theater with an amazing roar. No one complained.

Tripping over their own feet, a heterosexual couple (making as much noise as a regiment) chose to sit directly behind me, making the seats creak. As the lion roared, they started to talk. With the opening credits, they stopped for a moment. Then, the guy whispered something in the girl's ear and she started laughing and he (provocateur provoked) chimed in. I turned my head sideways (in such cases, an immediate display of annoyance can sometimes make the perpetrators of the annoyance alter their behavior) and tightened my lips in a grimace that attempted to convey the displeasure they were causing me.

With the exception of the creaking of the seats, for a while there was silence (I wasn't sure if my pantomime had had its desired effect or if, in fact, it was due to chance), but I soon heard the loud rustle of cellophane. Beyond any doubt, it was candy being unwrapped and the noise (in the near-emptiness of the theater) dominated everything. It seemed as if the sound track of the film had gone silent and the scratch-scratch of the endless cellophane were emerging from the very loudspeakers. No sooner was the first piece of candy unwrapped than the girl's voice said, "Do you want one?" The boy's "Yes" was already blending with the opening bars of the new cellophane symphony. One after another, they unwrapped seven candies. Then they were still.

The movie was all dry landscapes—up one panorama and down the next. The action was finally now beginning. The stranger had walked into the bar and everyone was eyeing him askance. He asked for a whiskey and the bartender served him begrudgingly. A bleary-eyed man with a beard was picking his teeth.

Suddenly, the girl behind me sneezed. And what had seemed like an isolated incident—a too-early harbinger of spring—was to become an endless recital (mixed in with four clicks of the snap

on her handbag) which came to an end when the girl, on blowing her nose, offered a noteworthy demonstration of nasal wind,
from which I was distracted by the smell of toasted corn.

If there is one smell in this world that I detest, it is the smell
of toasted corn. No one was eating any, however, neither to
my right nor to my left, and the happy couple was too busy un-
wrapping candy to go on to more tacky fare. The thought escaped me in a loud voice: "What's going on?"

From the row in front of me (which until that moment had
seemed empty) a little man popped up his little head and looked
at me with tiger eyes: "Enough already with the noise, okay?"

I was about to respond that I had merely been the author of
the last utterance, and that, innocent of all the sounds and smells,
it was not I who ought to be chastised. In mid-word, however,
three more heads turned, obliging me to keep my peace.

I got up. I found another seat two or three rows farther down,
on the other side of the aisle. Now I could no longer understand a thing that was happening on the screen. Four scoundrels
who looked like cardsharps (one of them was the stranger from
before) were playing poker. It seemed that one of them had been
dealt a full house: three aces and a pair of jacks. This clearly
surprised the stranger, who himself had a pair of aces, which
could only mean that there were five aces on the table, a definitely abnormal circumstance if we bear in mind that they were
playing with just one deck. It was thus evident that one of the
two was cheating. As each of them protested his innocence and
called the other guilty, the affair turned into a quick gun duel,
the winner of which turned out to be the stranger, to the dismay of the local boys; nevertheless, they carried off the corpse
and looked for a replacement to continue with the game. They
dropped one of the copycat aces from the deck and went on
playing. The mess started up again when two more players (this
time, the stranger was an amused onlooker), convinced of the
quality of the cards that fortune had dealt them, started up-
ping the ante, higher and higher. They were both so sure of their
hands that each bet his last penny. When they showed their
cards it turned out that both of them had aces-high poker.

If, for one ace too many, a duel had occurred, for two aces-high hands, a slaughter must certainly be in store. Not so, however. Before an argument could even begin, one of the two potential adversaries had already shot the other down, which immediately established his innocence. They looked for another new replacement and demanded a new deck.

For a moment I considered whether it might not be a good time to leave. If the lugubriousness of the theater weren't enough, the picture was a total loss. And the music was repetitious, the actors had no idea what they were doing. . . . Now they had resumed playing, and aces appeared on all sides. They changed decks several times until, thoroughly burned, they started popping off bullets left and right. Only one player was left alive: the stranger, who was now getting up and walking into the foreground, as if the mere fact of having survived destined him for higher enterprises, a conclusion not even he believed. Two rows down, a kid laughed, unwrapped a piece of newspaper, and pulled out a sandwich. Tuna fish. I could smell it.

Except for the owner of the bar it appeared that the entire village had died in the carnage. The stranger was drinking now, propped up at the bar, not knowing what to do (more or less in affinity with the director of the movie). The shot went on for endless minutes, the stranger downing glass after glass, as if hoping for one of us to toss him an idea so he could go on with the action. How could this mess continue? I was less and less interested in finding out. From a wall of the theater, a globe-shaped light fixture fell to the floor and broke into a thousand shards. A laugh rang out.

Then I felt someone touching my thigh. Taken by surprise, I didn't know how to react. It was the first time anyone had ever tried to touch me in a movie house. I didn't dare turn my head and see who the stealthy individual trying to feel me up was; the seat next to mine had been empty when I sat down. I wasn't sure whether it was a man or a woman (the weight of the hand was little clue), but whoever it was, I imagined a twisted body, a pimply face. . . . Most likely, it was an androgyne, an androgyne from outer space. I saw it as green, with a mouth full of steely teeth. Perhaps the wisest solution would be to pay it no mind and, in the face of my indifference, the hand would disappear as stealthily as it had arrived. I tried to give my full attention to the screen—the stranger was now dancing with a dance hall girl whose hairdo was too modern—but that was no solution. The hand continued to advance. I took a deep breath and turned. It was the woman from the box office who was kneading my thigh, thereby assuming her third role in that establishment. Or was she acting on her own initiative? From a few rows behind came a solid crash. A seat had collapsed, and everyone laughed, even the victim, who was now getting up from the floor and dust ing himself off. The woman from the box office laughed too, and then said to me in a low voice:

"Don't get upset. Do you like the movie? I've seen it so many times I know it by heart. Did you know that today was our last day? I've never seen you around here before. New faces really stand out here. We've been seeing the same ones for years now. We see one another so often it's as if we never aged. You see that couple? They've been coming every day for years, and they always sit in the same spot. Do you like the movie? It's not very good, to tell the truth. Of all the pictures we've shown— and there have been many!—the one I liked the best was one we projected when this hall only offered first-run movies. This used to be a premiere movie house years ago, you know! It was such a pretty movie and it ended just as it had begun. The projectionist, who was younger then, perhaps, ran it in such a way that it seemed as if the movie never ended, and it lasted for three or four showings without stopping. It's a good thing we had to stop, late at night. If not he would have made it go on for days—and maybe we'd still be there. The protagonist was a young man who wanted to flee his destiny . . . as if you could flee from what has been written! Now, in fact, I can't quite re- member the story. I know there was a shadowy mansion, full of fog, and a stage set crumbling with age. There was also a girl, but I don't know what she was there for. He fled from the house, I think, but ended up going back, because no matter where he went he carried destruction with him and, whether in the

subway or a summer house on the shore, everything quickly fell
to ruin about him. I don't remember it too well, but the lesson
seems clear to me: No one can escape his future. Mmmm. . . .
Do you want to leave? Why don't you stay. Later on we'll cel-
ebrate the last movie. Now it's as if you were one of the family."

I got up. Some nights it's better to stay home. There were pieces
missing from the chessboard. I walked up the aisle without looking back. The couple with the candy laughed as they watched
me. Every few feet, seats were gone, and the rows looked like
dentures with missing teeth. In the last row, a couple was wrapped
in an outrageous embrace. From the door to the bathroom
emerged disturbing yelps. A masked thief assaulted the usher with
a huge knife. As I searched for the exit among the folds of
thick burgundy velvet drapes, I heard a loud crackling sound.
The screen had split diagonally, from top to bottom and from
right to left. Everyone burst out laughing.

Outside the rain had stopped. I walked quickly. I was afraid,
but I wasn't sure of what. A vague shadow, an evil fate that
(of this I was sure) would linger on until the sun came out. If I
managed to see the morning, I would be safe. All the way home,
I stepped only on every other crack. When I got to my house I
discovered that I didn't have my keys. I had lost them or they
had been stolen (by the woman from the box office?). "So," I
said to myself, "*voilà*, your evil fate." But I wasn't convinced.
In the pit of my stomach, I felt that worse things were yet to
come that night. I could, of course, call the fire department to
break down the door. But that was no solution. Sooner or later
I'd have to face it. If I didn't go to them, they'd come to me.
The thought of reporting them made me laugh. I'd find them at
the police station, dressed as the commissioner, the cops, a
masked bandit apparently under arrest, the woman from the box
office playing the warden. . . . The meowing of a cat made me
cry out.

I began to retrace my steps back to the movie house. I thought:
when I get there they'll all be waiting for me, laughing sul-
phurous laughs and clanking keys dangling from their hands. I
thought: When I get there, the demolition team will already

have begun to tear down the building and I won't be able to
find a single one of those sinister personages. I will know that
a terrible curse has fallen upon me forever more.... At the corner, though, there were my keys, lying on the sidewalk, glint-
ing like diamonds. As I picked them up, I thought: Now I don't
have to go back. I thought: The sooner I get there, the sooner
it will all be over. I thought: Have I gone mad? Am I afraid of
ghosts?

I wished fervently that the sun would come out.

THE VEGETABLE KINGDOM

From the grandchild of Uncle Ximo
to the grandchild of Matons

To SAY THAT TIMES ARE HARD IS TO SAY NEXT TO NOTHING, IS to speak in clichés; it is to say nothing at all. We have all used the expression so often that it has lost its meaning, if indeed it ever had one; times have always been hard for clichés. Perhaps it is more precise to say that we have lost our course; worse still, we doubt there is a course (and, in consequence, we doubt there is a discourse, the necessary subversion of the former), and everything is shifting, changing, like shadows in a high school corridor. They say these are times of crisis, and I like to think that this is why everything is going awry. Because (if this theory holds water), when the crisis is over, the compasses will once again begin to function. Some years ago, we thought we had it all figured out; we had dashed the idols to the ground (but not all idols; therein, perhaps, our error), and we set ourselves upon pedestals, in the hope that two and two would no longer be four. Defenestrations have always made do, if not much more, as a course. Now we are adults (we have learned that two thrashings plus two thrashings equal four thrashings) and we wonder whether to continue atop the pedestals, put some of the idols back in place, share the absurdity with them, or leap headlong into the void—leave it all behind and allow the pedestals to decay into barbarous savannahs where, in days to come, someone will have something to say and will forge new statues (of plastic, we trust, the better for burning and creating a stink).

I have always been depraved. My generation (perhaps degeneration would be a better word; we have been a fortunately degenerate generation) was born in the shadow of the early Stones and the disputes between mods and rockers. We projected our ire onto every possible plane (or sphere, as they said at one symposium or another) of social orthodoxy. Rationally, sensibly (and these words, in this context, take on a new meaning) we came to understand that heterodoxy and depravity were synonyms not entered in any dictionary.

I said that I was (and am) depraved, but I have not defined how. (I don't know if I can: I can see the roots clearly enough, but from there on everything turns into lost evolutionary stages.) At the Enfants Terribles, we fraternized with broken-down whores, Brazilian and Yankee sailors, North Africans (as they're calling them now) of the kind who wear sunglasses at midnight. We learned ethics with them. We became cynical and opportunistic, and when the first hippies disembarked on our beaches, we knew we'd never get on with them. Turning the other cheek was not our style; we denied our sentiments (and we were sentimental to a fault), and the only goals that urged us on were those that would redound in some benefit to us. Time has proved us not to have been entirely wrong: Nowadays the hippies are a dead issue and the opportunists have taken over.

With the seventies, the real fireworks began. The defenders of the ethics of perversion revealed themselves to be highly un-

ethical and perversely unperverse—opportunists, period. I had my
fill of junkies and small-timers, and the new generations of ac-
tivists (ecologists, macrobioticists, and conscientious objectors) made
my stomach turn.

As a rebel (that is, as a teenager), I had been a skirt chaser,
indefatigable, but sweet. I need not explain, however, that the
day comes when a man tires of everything. And when I said
day, I might as well have said night, for that night I was reading Baudelaire, stretched out in the hammock on the balcony,
surrounded by dwarf palms and hydrangeas, facing a yellow
moon that smiled over the blue bay. Txitxi was pacing up and
down inside the apartment, bored, sober, sad, unerotic; she didn't
want to drink, she didn't want to talk, and above all, she didn't
want to fuck. Perhaps even more bored than she, I got up from
the hammock, took her by the arm, and twisted it until she
screamed and started crying (looking at me with eyes that con-
fessed that suddenly her boredom had vanished). Cleansed of any
burden to my conscience, I forced her: I had written the first
entry in my vita of perversions. As in a miracle, I was suddenly
illuminated and I felt woozy from the light that swept me up.
I discovered, all at once, that I had been vegetating for years. I
was now a bear awakening after a long hibernation and about to
choose the path that seemed most worthy: I would become a classic
libertine. I should taste only of those fruits that were forbidden.
In time, I began specializing in girls: a question of age.

From then on, everything went smoothly. I don't know if you've
heard it said that vice is a spiral that expands in all directions;
the shifting sands suck you in never to release you. At first, en-
couraged by my initial experience, I became a rapist. (The first
few times the pleasure was mixed with a certain regret, but thereafter I spent no time on such sentimental nonsense.) Finally,
aware of the importance of my work in a society such as ours, I
decided to study the theoretical problem of which functions I
should have to fulfill, in the event that rather than playing the
role of the corruptor, I should not simply have fallen into a
state of corruption. And as theoretical reflection can never bear
fruit unless accompanied by a conscientious praxis, I became
(alternately, consecutively, simultaneously) an exhibitionist, a voyeur,

a perverter of minors, a gigolo, a sadist, a bestialist, a masochist, a pederast. Terrain forbidden to me was terrain that came under my siege. No aberration is strange to me. For this reason, when I say that times are hard, I say it knowing full well whereof I speak, the product (as I have stated) of a program of study at once both theoretical and practical.

I shall now bring you up to date: Wednesday, at one-thirty a.m., I was at the Whisky Twist. Propped up on the bar by my elbows, I was smoking, contemplating the shelfful of bottles and trying to read the labels, anonymous as they were in the blue and red lights of the bar. There were couples dancing in the back. On the street, two people were slugging it out and each punch sent one of the two flying against the door of the bar, until the bouncer went out and put an end to the show. I ordered a drink, but I don't know what or from whom. I only remember (and I cannot remember more because it seems as if everything that happened later has erased my memory of preceding events) that when I turned to look toward the dance floor, I saw her sitting two or three stools down.

She was drinking an odd, orangey drink. She had long, dark hair, which she wore loose around the shoulders. In profile, she reminded me of a dark Sylvie Vartan.

She was wearing a jeans jacket of the kind you don't see anymore (short, Levi's), faded like her pants. I don't know now if, on first seeing her sweet face, which looked like a map of innocence, I saw her as an attractive morsel to be added to my history of infamy, or if I was shocked (me, moved?) to find, after so many years, a girl dressed as we used to dress a decade earlier. She reminded me of a girlfriend I had picked up one night at the Jazz Colón, when the Jazz Colón was still the Jazz Colón and picking oneself up a girlfriend was still picking oneself up a girlfriend: flirting with her, captivating her, fucking her, and abandoning her, all in three quarters of an hour. This girl reminded me of Sunday afternoon get-togethers, the twist, the madison, someone's parents always just about to get home from the movies. She reminded me of the Shadows, Jerry Lee Lewis, Michel Polnareff; she reminded me of myself beside myself with love for a girl with freckles.

I took a roundabout approach. My opening was so subtle that I wondered if it wasn't precisely this first move in the chess game that so surprised her that she let down her guard in confusion. (Nowadays, the way things work, "yes" and "no" have no mystery to them, they are immediate and definite.) We talked of trivialities, we walked around the Born, we had hot chocolate near the park, we walked up the Rambla: I left her at the door to her house without having so much as touched a hair on her head, but with her telephone number in my pocket. So far was I from depravity that I looked more like a guardian angel out to earn Brownie points. It was frightening to think I could even go so far as to feel good—that kind of good— playing that docile role. Back home, I felt called upon to masturbate over photographs of animals (pigs, dogs, and donkeys) penetrating damsels with dyed blond hair; after all, my moral integrity had to be preserved. I tacked up the phone number by the phone; I would call her the next day. Now I was calm. It was quite clear that I was a cad and that she was just one more notch on my belt. I fell asleep thinking just how cruel and dissipated I would be acting in a few short hours.

I had no difficulty in arranging a meeting. At my very own home, immediately; such had been my performance as a gentleman the previous night! I offered her drinks and drugs. She chose a fruit juice and as two boxers on television had it out for the European welterweight championship, I began to kiss her neck and nibble at her throat. For a moment, she acted surprised and I felt ridiculous; perhaps she had seriously taken me for a milquetoast. I spent enough time on her mouth so that, when I went on to her breasts (vanilla ice cream with strawberry nipples) she could no longer say no to anything. On the television screen, one of the boxers was waving triumphantly and the other was still on the floor, kayoed. The news came on. A half hour later they were going to show a film I've always liked, *A Streetcar Named Desire*, with Marlon Brando and Vivien Leigh. I didn't want to miss it, so I decided to finish up with the girl before it began. Something told me she would put up some resistance, and that put an edge on my desire. When I began to undress her, her protestations had been feeble, but the struggle

to remove her skirt became herculean, as if suddenly her honor
were at stake. You figure it. But this was intriguing. Finally a
rape, *stricto sensu*, after so long. (Today's adolescents, who put
up no resistance, take away one's taste for the little pleasures of
life.) I found myself obliged to use force. On the floor, supine
and skirtless, she pressed her legs together and, flustered, string-
ing together one lie after another, begged my pardon and proposed any mode of compensation with the exception of the vaginal,
the buccal, or the anal: simply not licentious enough for me. I
ripped off her satin panties and attempted to slip a finger inside,
but something weird was going on. I opened the lips with care
(and this took a titanic effort, for those lips wouldn't give an inch;
it was as if they had a life of their own), and when I tried to
place a finger in her vagina, I saw that it was impossible: the
hole was sealed, impervious in a way previously unknown to
me. I assumed that she was capable of exercising an extraordi-
nary control over her vaginal muscles and was now doing so
in order to impede my entrance. I threatened to go look for a
drill. Terrified, she began to speak. I ought not to have listened; that was what did me in. Here and now I can still not
say whether or not she tricked me; or whether she is tricking
me still. She said:

"Wait. Don't think that this is bad faith on my part. Though
it may seem impossible to you, there is a real problem im-
peding your entrance. I am and am not responsible for this. I'd
have to go back many years in order to explain it all to you,
but I'll get right to the point: I have always been a woman
of very strong convictions. It's hard to explain. It is not only
that, as a child, the mere doubt as to whether I had a cold or
not brought on the most dreadful flu—that would even seem
reasonable. Nor is it the fact that, one day, playing cowboys and
Indians with my brother, I became so deeply convinced of my
role as a Sioux maiden that, for three days, I did nothing more
than ululate ritual ceremonies that filled my family with fear,
finally reaching the point at which I understood nothing but the
Sioux tongue—and when I say *nothing*, I mean just that: I was
not just pretending not to understand. I could give you countless
examples along these lines. I'll spare you the details. Mine is

a case that goes far beyond hypochondria or psychosomatic ten-
dencies. Stop looking at me like that; it pains me. I'm not lying
to you. When I get an idea into my head, it sweeps both me and
my volition away; it's stronger than either of us. A year ago, I
began to take an interest in vegetarianism and the minute I was
convinced of the virtues of such a regimen, things started moving in a direction I hadn't anticipated: I was totally convinced:
totally. What I mean by this is that I am a vegetarian from
head to toe and that my lips (all six of them—majora, minora,
and facial) will accept only organic fare. And I can do nothing
to remedy this situation until I can convince myself that vegetarianism is harmful or get it through my head that the fact that
it's healthful doesn't mean I must practice it."

Frankly, I fell for it. I was moved by that splendid body
trembling in my arms and I believed her. My entire moral castle fell to the ground in no time flat. I was no longer a tower of
incorruptible depravity; for once I let understanding win me
over. And in a big way: not only did I not force her, but in order to keep her satisfied I plied her with cucumbers, carrots,
eggplants . . . she says she loves me dearly. The gynecologist
says it's a case for the psychologist. The psychologist says it's
all a question of getting her to believe that vegetarianism is per-
nicious. Because it really seems that for her there are no gray
areas. Everything is black or white; either she's totally convinced
of something or entirely disbelieving. If I manage to convince
her of the virtues of perversity, my ship will be in: Since vegetarianism is anything but perverse, she will end up rejecting it.
She seems disposed to letting herself be convinced. She's beginning to understand my quirks and they even seem to appeal to
her—to such an extent that she's reading the works of the Mar-
quis with greater delight than her manuals on cabbages and
radishes. I shall not mince words: Yesterday a thought began to
obsess me. What if she takes such an interest in depravity that
she becomes *totally* perverse and, scorpion and pygmalion all in
one, decides that the maximum perversion to which she can
aspire is to turn (in some unforeseeable way) her poisonous tail
toward me?

OLDEBERKOOP

To Marcelo Cohen, *xava gamba.*

WHEN IS IT GOING TO STOP SNOWING? I HAVE TO FIND A WAY out of here. How long have we been here? Eleven days, at least. Or is it ten? Ten or eleven—I've lost count. And you're not keeping track—you who said that the snow wouldn't last long because it had just rained, so it wasn't going to stick! Well, God knows what would happen if it really stuck. Things get started over nothing and then get bigger and bigger until they swallow you up. What is it you're writing? We're all so serious here. All these people are so serious that they resort to drunkenness with terrifying ease. When they get smashed, they scare me, and they get smashed so often it's hard to believe that there's any alcohol left! I have to get out. Those people who speak that strange language are cute; but we still don't know what

they're speaking. It's obviously not Dutch. And they don't look
Indonesian. Maybe they're Frisian? Have you ever heard Frisian?
Maybe that's it. You say they're speaking Hebrew, but if they
were speaking Hebrew they'd be Israelis and all Israelis speak
English as a second language, and these guys know about as
much English as ... so many days here and we still don't know.
I'd like to be able to talk with them, ask them things. I'd ask
them where they're from, how they live, what they do, what their
interests are. I'd ask them about everything. I've already told
you this a dozen times, but I can't help it. Nothing has happened here in ten or eleven days ... or is it twelve? (You want
a drag?) I feel like talking. You know me; when I'm not busy, I
can't stop talking. (You know there's no more milk?) Of course
you know, I told you just a while ago. And I told you just a while
ago because you told me this morning. But let me tell you something, okay? Even if you already know it and, in point of fact, it
isn't really news. Mmmm. If I had a new kitchen I'd put green
tiles in it, just like these. Don't you want a toke? What are you
writing? Mmmmmm. Hey! What's all that clanging? Must be
that kid. (What's his name ... Jan?) From the racket that's going
down he must have destroyed all the china, at very least. He's
awfully nervous, that kid. You hear what they're saying now? It
must be a lot of fun. Don't you hear them? Why're you looking at me like that? Mmmm. This is really good stuff. Where
do you think they got it from? There wasn't a trace of weed
in the place, and now all of a sudden there's a whole stash. That
skinny stuck-up guy must have been holding out. I don't like
him; he looks like a creep. Thank them. Hey, thanks! Mmmmm,
it's so ... how should I put it? (Oh, who cares ...) And to
think that I have some at home, all planted—a whole row of
flowerpots. Pot in pots. And Maria must be smoking it all.
Mmmm. Don't tell me you don't know her. Maria is quite a character. She never has a dime in her pocket, but she's always
known which wine to order— you know the kind of person I
mean. I like people who have that touch. It would be heaven
if someone here had some acid. Maybe the snob ... have you
ever done acid? You have? That's a surprise. How about mushrooms? I'll bet anything you've never tried mushrooms, right?

No, of course not. Mushrooms are ... so ... it's like ... it's
like a movie. You feel as though you're in a Walt Disney picture;
the sky, deep blue and fake, like a stage set, and yet ever so real ...
As if the whole world were a set, full of artificial light ... green
grass ... It's not like acid, dummy. You're really out there. I've
never done any hard drugs, none at all. They get you on slippery
ground, and if you slip you can fall all the way in. Listen, is snow
heroin, like horse, or is it coke? How ironic to be talking about
snow now, surrounded by the stuff. We could go out and shoot it
all up (or sniff it, whichever you prefer); then we'd be able to get
out of here in a hurry. Tell that fat guy over there; he looks
like a junkie. I once had a boyfriend who did heroin and it was
a problem because he could never get it up, and the way I am,
when there's something that can't be done, I feel like doing it
even more. Imagine it. I was out of my mind to fuck him and
it was out of the question ... When I met you, you were a real
sight! I thought you were stoned. Then it turned out you
weren't; that's just your natural state. Mmmm ... you see? I told
you so—as soon as it started snowing I told you we should get
out of here. At very least, now we'd be in the next village, in
some little hotel, in bed, having chamomile and honey ... What
did the owner say? Poor devil, little did he know he'd be having
overnight guests in his bar. If they had rooms, it wouldn't matter. Anyway, after this experience we could start our own hotel.
What did he just say? He must have asked whose turn it is
to help in the kitchen. It's not ours, right? He hasn't even
looked at us ... One night I had to sleep in a bar. Have I ever
told you that story? At Pito's bar. Have you ever been there?
The place is too noisy and smoky, with a TV that never stops—
and that nobody watches—and one of those pinball machines with
lots of letters and numbers that blink on and off and on and
off. If you ever head for it with the intention of playing a game,
Pito dashes over and runs his dust rag along the glass on top
of the machine (thereby managing to keep you from seeing the
ball), and elbows you left and right (whereby—if by this time
you had still been able to stay in control of the game—the ball
finally drops out of sight). Pito is crazy. He's a grouch and a
gentleman all in one. If you ask him for a beer, he serves you

Coca-Cola, and if you ask for a coffee with cognac he serves
you a cuba libre or a rum screwdriver, and if you ask for a rum
screwdriver he brings you a dish of tripe or an egg cream, all
the while either ranking you out, looking askance at you, intro-
ducing you to the guy next to you at the bar, or yelling at the
dog, which has a real sad face and looks more and more like
Pito every day. (Both of them belong to the same original and
unique species, which bears more of a kinship to coffee and
cognac than to man or dog . . .) The night I had to stay over, I
finally figured out that what you had to do was never ask for
what you really wanted or for whatever was apparently the opposite of what you wanted. In the end, you could get Pito to
serve, if not exactly what you wanted, at least something similar. I wanted a whiskey, so I asked for stuffed olives and an
orange drink. He served me a cognac and a sweet-roll. I drank
the cognac and left the sweet-roll on the bar. I wasn't too far
off. With the second order, I went farther astray. I still felt like
having a whiskey, so I asked for a tonic water. He served me a
dry sherry, a drink I despise. On the third try, I hit the jack-
pot. I asked for raspberry syrup with seltzer, and I got a splendid malt whiskey (straight up—hallelujah!) in a shot glass filled
to the brim. Throughout all these stratagems, it was raining out,
much more than cats and dogs. It was raining as it has *never*
before rained on this planet; to call it a flood would be to di-
minish considerably the proportions of the event. No one had
the slightest notion of going home, not even those who lived just
a couple of doors down. The people trapped there were, therefore, quite a heterogeneous bunch. We started card games that
we had to suspend at two in the morning in order to move
up to the second floor because the ground floor had been completely flooded. We went on playing until 5:30 in the morning,
when the rain slowed and some of us headed home, others off
to work. Hardly a drop had fallen anywhere else in the city.
These things are strange. Maybe that's what's happening here,
and in the next town it's not even snowing. It's only snowing
at this bend in the road and nowhere else in the world. Maybe
we'll use up all the snow and it will never snow again, *per om-
nia saecula saeculorum*; and our children and grandchildren won't

ever know what snow is. Did you notice that the snow has covered almost a foot of the window? Do you think it will break?
Why don't you tell the owner to close the shutters? Otherwise the snow will break the glass. Besides, it won't be so cold
then. How come no one thought of that till now? Look. Now
it's snowing even harder. Look how the snow against the window
is rising—faster than ever. There. You can't see the sky anymore; you can't see anything—just snow. Soon we'll be out of
air. It will snow so hard we'll disappear, and so will the build-
ings—all under a blanket of snow. And we'll die of asphyxi-
ation when the air is all used up, which won't be long now, and
it will be so cold that the snow will never melt and after man-
kind adapts to the new Ice Age (that must be it, we've entered a
new era; we've gone back millions of years in time!), they will
build highways on top of us. And a thousand years from now,
nearsighted archaeologists will find our cadavers in a state of
perfect preservation; like in a refrigerated storage room. They'll
undress us, they'll observe us, they'll do tests on us ... How
awful! Why haven't any snowplows showed up yet? Things like
this must be commonplace in this country—maybe not this
much snow, of course, but they must be used to snowstorms.
Why don't they come and fix the telephone? Mmmmm. Here.
It's almost all gone—all but the roach. What time is it? If
only the TV worked, at least ... Why do these things always
have to happen to us? Phew, I'm sleepy. Will you come and stretch
out with me, over in the corner? Could we take a nap, please?
You—always writing. As if you didn't know how to do anything else. What good does it do you? What are you writing,
if you don't mind my asking? Let's see ... you're out of your
mind. Why are you writing down everything I say? I see. You're
not even inventing what you write. I can order you to write one
thing or another, and you'll only be able to write what I decide upon. Write shit. *Shit.* No, I was just reading it. Hey, stop.
You're crazy. Write just what I tell you to wri— Hey! You
wrote half a word; good. If I stop talking now, you won't write
anything. Will you leave a blank space or write a period? Let's
see ... Phooey. You've written suspension points. That's not very
original; you've done that before. Don't you ever start a new

paragraph? Start a new paragraph. Now. It pisses me off that you're ignoring me. You write so as not to talk. You think you're above it all and you're just a little shit, like all the rest. Do you think I like being here? You could be a little more pleasant. Communication between people is interesting—if nothing more. Haven't you ever thought about that? Look into my eyes. Look at me. Don't write *look at me* and look at me. No. Don't write *Don't write* look at me *and look at me* and look at me. No. Don't write *No. Don't write* don't write *look at me* and look at me *and look at me* and look at me. Oh, the hell with it. Now I'll stop talking so you'll stop writing and look at me—or get bored. *Non scriverai più.*